"Barbara Bretton is simply the best storyteller ever...."

—Bertrice Small, author of
Love, Remember Me

"Spend the weekend with me."

Stefanie's hand moved back from his.

"I know it sounds crazy, but don't pull away." Dan's voice was husky, yet the rougher edges were smoothed over by desire.

His fingers curled around her hand and she couldn't stop her own fingers from clasping his in response. His eyes held her in thrall and she was powerless to break the spell that had suddenly—magically—surrounded them.

But she must.

"Dan...I can't."

"Why not?"

"I hardly know you."

His laugh was low and appealingly uncertain.

"After this weekend you would."

Barbara Bretton will "... warm your heart, tickle your funny bone and leave you begging for more."

—*Romantic Times*

BARBARA BRETTON

NO SAFE PLACE

MIRA BOOKS

ISBN 1-55166-044-X

NO SAFE PLACE

MIRA and the star colophon are trademarks of MIRA Books.

Printed in U.S.A.

For my grandparents,
Elsie Newton and Loren McNutt—
for telling me stories
I never forgot...

and

For Elda Minger,
who understands (better than most)
the importance of it all

1

Stefanie Colt lifted her hand to brush a strand of auburn hair back from her cheek and to take a discreet peek at her wristwatch. The conference room where she'd been barricaded since lunchtime had been darkened for a slide presentation and she had to bring her wrist closer to her face and squint in order to make out the time.

Next to her Gabe Freeman chuckled low. "Want to make a break for it, Colt?" he stage-whispered.

"I don't dare," she whispered back. She turned to face the young man whose easy grin hid an ambition that was taking him to the top in record time. "They probably have guard dogs at the door."

"Trust me." Gabe took Stefanie's hand and stood up. "I've been told I have a way with guard dogs and wild women."

She grabbed her briefcase from the floor and followed him from the darkened room, thankful she had picked a seat in the last row for the slide presentation on the new Conway News Service facilities in Honolulu. She glanced quickly around the auditorium, relaxing a little when she saw everyone's eyes glued with corporate devotion to the screen in the front of the room.

It wasn't like Stefanie to miss even the most boring of her client's presentations, but lately she'd been having a difficult time performing the most routine duties. All she could think of at that moment was how long a walk it was from the building to the security of her car, of just how deserted and dark the parking lot would be when she finally left.

Gabe held the swinging door open for her and she slipped past him into the brightly lit corridor.

"Nothing worse than corporate home movies," he said as the door swung shut behind the two of them.

Stefanie chuckled and stretched her narrow shoulders, adjusting the cutaway jacket of her jade green linen suit. "I'll admit they nearly lost me with the Conway Five Commandments. It made me glad I only work with Conway, not for."

Gabe's dark brown eyes danced behind his metal-rimmed glasses. "The old man was going to go for Ten Commandments until Harry told him someone beat him to it."

Her laugh echoed in the empty corridor. Stefanie seldom laughed these days and the sound took both of them by surprise.

"Keep it down, Colt," Gabe said, inclining his head toward the closed door. "Guard dogs and wild women I can handle. Crazed execs I'm not so sure about."

"You underestimate yourself," she answered, grinning as he loosened the knot on his tie and ran a finger around the inside of his shirt collar. Gabe Freeman had been her contact at Conway News since her employer, Tele-Com International, a private phone company, had secured the account two years ago. "You drove a hard bargain on those overseas press relays," she continued as they strolled down the hallway toward the staircase. "Thanks to your proposal, I was able to convince Tele-Com to give you the preferred customer rate." Her green eyes sparkled as she broke the good news. "Two and a half percent across the board."

Gabe let out a whoop of excitement. "If this doesn't get me a bonus, I'll eat my hat."

"You don't wear a hat."

"Then I'll eat old man Conway's hat." He awkwardly patted Stefanie's shoulder, a gesture curiously gentle for such a burly man. "It never would have happened without you, Stef. Thanks."

She shrugged off his gratitude with a laugh and a flip remark; inside, however, she was very pleased with the outcome of the deal. Working as liaison between Conway and Tele-Com, she often felt she was privy only to problems and hassles. Only rarely did she have the chance to see her hard work result in something as tangible as the preferred customer rate Gabe had wanted so desperately.

He walked quickly and she had to adjust her stride to keep up with him. He took the stairs at breakneck speed and she gave up any pretense of trying to match his pace.

"If I'd known we were going jogging, I would have exchanged my pumps for Pumas," she said, leaning against the railing at the foot of the staircase and panting comically. "Don't you ever slow down?"

He shook his head no. "You of all people should know that. Who taught me all I know about using the fast lane?" he answered, his face serious for a change.

"You make me sound like Mother Time." She tried to keep her tone light, but the edge in it was unmistakable. "I'm only twenty-eight, Gabe."

"Yeah, but you've been at it for so long!" Gabe was not a man conditioned to recognizing subtleties of expression. "I mean, you graduated MIT and walked into an executive level job a week later. Beats the hell out of night school, I'll tell you that."

Stefanie said nothing. She had always been uncomfortable with the trappings of wealth, and her family's financial freedom was no secret. The Colt family of Boston and its environs was one of those early-American families who looked with suspicion on anyone arriving after the Pilgrims. Life to the Colts was a responsibility and a challenge, and they had programmed their only daughter with the same rigidity and zeal with which they had programmed their sons. By the time she turned twenty-four she was already in the fast lane Gabe had spoken about. It was only recently she'd begun to look for an exit ramp.

"I feel like a high school kid playing hooky," she said as she and Gabe strolled, at a slower pace, down the hallway toward the employees' dining room on ground level. "How much time do we have before we ought to get back to the conference?"

"About a half hour." Gabe's chuckle was low and rumbly. "I've seen that film four times already. They still have to sit through aerial views of Waikiki as seen from the penthouse, and several cute shots of the boss *en famille.*"

They paused at the door of the game room and listened to the beeps and siren sounds coming from the assortment of video games inside. "Best three out of five in Donkey Kong?" she asked.

Gabe groaned. "The way you massacred me last time?" He shook his head, a lock of light brown hair drooping over his high forehead. "Forget it. I've already bowed to superiority. How about a quick cup of coffee instead?"

Now she groaned. "Okay, but I'll warn you—I went into caffeine overdrive a few hours ago. From here on I won't be responsible for my disposition."

Gabe stopped in front of the door to the cafeteria. "I've seen you in one of your famous bad tempers," he said, his broad face split by a smile. "That's nothing new to me."

"Some friend you are." Stefanie playfully socked him in the forearm. "Friends are supposed to ignore friends' shortcomings."

He laughed. "I'm a friend, Stef, not a fool!"

She ran a hand through her just-above-the-shoulder-length auburn hair. "Listen, you grab us a table while I freshen up. I'll be back in a moment."

Gabe nodded then ducked into the cafeteria as she turned and hurried down the hallway toward the ladies' room. The sounds from the game room had faded and her only accompaniment now was the click of her high heels against the white-tiled floor and the rapid pounding of her heart. She rounded the corner and paused to glance out the large window that looked out on the parking lot. Now familiar apprehensions tugged along the base of her spine. The sky had already darkened to the bluish-smoke color of dusk and all that remained of the sun was a fierce orange glow behind the other office buildings in the Conway News Service complex. The thought of the long drive home on the unlighted Long Island highways made her heart climb up into her throat and threatened to close off her breathing.

Don't think about it, she told herself. *Put it out of your mind.* At first she'd been able to do that; shock had provided a cushion. As time went on, however, she found herself becoming more reluctant to go on the many business trips her dual responsibilities for Conway and Tele-Com demanded. Her boundaries were shrinking as her fears grew, and that frightened her more than anything else.

She turned abruptly from the window and dashed into the ladies' room.

A few minutes later, her wavy hair arranged carefully around her face and her makeup freshened, she came out of the lavatory and was about to head back to the cafeteria when the sounds of laughter and the unmistakable thud of a human form hitting the floor came from the gymnasium across the hall.

A man's voice, deep and commanding, rose above the laughter. "I'm going to throw punches," he said. "Block what you see. Now!"

The accent was unmistakable.

As had been pointed out to her thousands of times in the six years she'd been working in New York, no one on earth sounds quite like a Bostonian. Her own voice still carried the flavor and feel of her hometown.

Gabe and the meeting she should be returning to drifted out of her mind, replaced by an intense curiosity about the owner of that voice. The door was partly open and she kept her body shielded from view while she peeked inside the gym.

Stefanie had expected to find a basketball game in progress or a legion of runners racing around an indoor track. Instead the room was awash in a sea of white-pajamaed women who alternately blocked invisible punches with first their right arms, then their left. The last thing she had expected to find was a karate class in full swing, and the whole spectacle struck her as so comical that she pressed a hand over her mouth to stifle a laugh.

She poked her head in a little farther, hoping to get a glimpse of the owner of the voice. Each time one of the students would block with the wrong arm, that deep male voice would call out, "Don't let it throw you. Keep going. You'll get it . . . Fine . . . that's great. Now go into your stretches. You know the routine."

Bare feet slapped against the polished wood floor and she retreated farther back into the shadows of the hallway as the sound came closer. They stopped near the door and she held her breath, pushing herself ever deeper into the shadows.

"No sense standing out there all alone. Why don't you join us?"

"I'm not a voyeur, I promise you," she said as she reluctantly stepped into the light of the open door to meet the owner of the voice. "I—I was heading back down the hall when I thought I heard a noise and I stopped to investigate." It took all of her hard-earned self-possession to keep from staring openly at the tanned chest revealed by the slashed front of the black karate pajamas, which suddenly didn't make her feel like laughing at all.

He looked something of the pirate as he stood before her in that exotic garb—dangerous, glorious, and very, very male.

"Interested in karate?" he asked, his smile exposing startlingly white teeth between a full black mustache and neatly trimmed beard.

She shook her head. Bluntness was both her virtue and her vice. "Not particularly, I'm afraid. All that chopping and slicing seems better suited to a cooking class than an exercise class."

He threw his head back and laughed. "You don't mince words, do you?"

Unconsciously touching the pearls at the base of her throat with one hand, she lifted her chin and met the challenge in his eyes. "Not if I feel someone is strong enough to stand the truth."

He raked a tanned hand through thick, curly black hair. The top of the karate outfit gaped open a slight bit more and she caught a glimpse of dark springy curls on his chest as well. "What makes you think I'm strong enough to stand the truth?" he continued, clearly enjoying the confrontation.

She let her hazel-green eyes travel lazily up his body, starting from the bare feet planted on the wooden floor, up the legs spread apart in a slightly aggressive stance, over a broad chest and wide shoulders to a face that, while not handsome, was so strong, so much the face of a man, that she felt herself growing light-headed with sudden desire. His eyes were so dark that in the half-light of the hallway she was hard put to tell if they were brown or deep blue.

"Well," she said, drawing her words out slowly, "if you're man enough to wear pajamas in public, then you're man enough to handle anything."

"The *gi,* or pajamas as you call them, is part of the discipline," he answered, not taking offense at her words. "They're for comfort. They also put everyone on an equal footing: There's no gender in this class. No male, no female—just students."

A grin she couldn't stop lit her narrow face. Before she could think, the words tumbled out. "I'd have no trouble telling your gender."

"I'll be damned," he said, his head inclined slightly toward her. "I think I've just been complimented."

"Don't let it go to your head," she answered, her voice calm and smooth, in direct opposition to her emotions. "A woman with a chest like yours would have one heck of a glandular problem."

He chuckled and she liked the sound. In fact, she liked the whole incredibly silly conversation they were having. It had been a long time since she'd felt so lighthearted, so carefree.

He shook his head. "What a combination. Not only the famous redhead temper, but a sense of humor. Lady, your type of woman is rare."

"Naturally," she said, tilting her chin a trifle higher. "I'm a limited edition."

"There's something to be said for—"

His words were stopped in midsentence.

"Dan! We're ready for the palm strikes now." The high sound of a woman's voice floated out from the gym.

"Colt! We've got to get back, pronto!" Gabe's voice boomed down the long corridor.

"I have to go..." they said simultaneously, then laughed.

"Do you work here?" he asked as he reluctantly moved back toward the gym.

"Yes," she answered, backing away down the hallway toward Gabe. "Well, not really, but I'm—"

"Stefanie! Get it in gear. They're waiting for us."

She started to say more but two of his students had pulled the pajamaed stranger back into the class and Gabe was thundering down on her, breathing smoke in the way only an up-and-coming executive can do.

Dan, she thought as she hurried down the hall, her high heels clattering against the tiled floor. *Dan what?*

He hadn't been quick enough. By the time he politely broke away from his class for the second time, she had disappeared down the hallway with the stocky man he recognized from the overseas department.

Stefanie.

Stefanie of the fiery hair.

He grinned and turned back to the class at hand.

Stefanie of the terrific legs.

He had no doubt he'd meet her again. He'd make sure of it. The second Stefanie reached Gabe, who was red-faced and rattled, he grabbed her hand and propelled her up the staircase and back to the conference room.

"Jennings tracked me down in the cafeteria," he said, voice ragged from the exertion of taking the stairs two at a time. "The system between L.A. and Tokyo went down an hour ago. With that big economic summit meeting starting tomorrow, Conway's ready to take a bite out of Tele-Com's hide." He glanced at Stefanie, whose soft features seemed to be hardening before his eyes in anticipation of battle. "I hope you brought your flak jacket with you—you're gonna need it."

She reluctantly let the image of Dan, delightful as it had been, dissolve. For now.

She shot Gabe an assessing glance. "Things are that bad?"

"That bad." His voice betrayed his anxiety. "I had to make up some story that you had a headache and had gone hunting down some Excedrin and I was trying to get you milk to coat your stomach."

"Thanks, Gabe, but you don't have to run interference for me. I can handle it."

He took his glasses off and rubbed the red spot on the bridge of his nose. "I'm glad you can, because I can't. I had to make up some excuse why I was lounging around the cafeteria with my feet propped up on a table, didn't I?"

She nodded, but her mind was already busy computing the list of technicians she would have to call, figuring out who would be available after hours on the Friday afternoon of Labor Day weekend.

As they rounded a corner toward the conference room, she couldn't resist glancing out once again at the parking lot. It was fully dusk now and night was rapidly approaching. A tiny crescent sliver of moon hovered near the expressway in the distance and the sight of the nearly deserted parking lot sent a jolt of fear through her that threatened to buckle her legs beneath her.

She'd been shirking her duties lately, cutting her hours short, not putting in the late nights she once had. She'd even been putting off flying out to the Coast to visit Tele-Com's home office because the thought of being that exposed to danger made her hands grow clammy.

Put it out of your mind, she commanded herself at the door to the conference room. She straightened her shoulders—thankful the padded suit jacket made them seem stronger and more capable than she felt at that moment—and entered. Conway and Al Jennings, his right-hand man, swept down on her with the righteous anger of avenging angels. There was no room at the moment for her fears.

"Don't panic, gentlemen," she said in her calm, clear Ivy League voice. "I'll have you set up again for business by nine P.M. You have my word."

In business she knew the rules: First you promise the impossible, then you do your damnedest to deliver it.

Stefanie got down to work.

From six thirty until eight forty-five she worked like a demon, juggling three phones at once, sending messages out on the Telex, making urgent pleas to electronics specialists, and, when necessary, calling in favors. Finally, by a few minutes before nine, she had eight of the fifteen lines between Los Angeles and Tokyo open for business, with the promise of full service by the next morning.

Conway Junior, the president of the overseas development department, had stayed on, quietly observing Stefanie's multiphone juggling act. His presence unnerved Gabe, who took his glasses on and off so many times to erase imaginary smudges that Stefanie was either going to offer to buy him a pair of contacts or else wind the wire-rimmed frames around his neck.

"Well, that's it," she said finally, a few moments after nine, when the confirmation call came in from Tokyo. "We have better than minimal service right now and everything will be in place when the summit begins." She reached behind her neck and absently rubbed the taut, tensed muscles.

Jack Conway stood up, walked toward her desk, and extended his hand. She stood and shook it.

"Great job, Colt. I'll see to it your superiors at Tele-Com hear about it."

She nodded her head in thanks. "I appreciate it, Jack. Have a good weekend."

Conway shrugged into his navy blazer and, with a nod toward Gabe who stood poised for flight near the door, hurried off for his holiday weekend.

Gabe shook his head when he heard the outer door swing open then closed. "Nice guy, isn't he? Not even a 'Thank you, Freeman. I know you're alive.'"

Stefanie felt a stab of sympathy for the younger man. "You've been around long enough to know the ropes, Gabe. You're never properly appreciated by your own company. Why do you think they say it's a jungle out there?"

He slid his glasses off his nose for the thousandth time and she restrained the scream that rose in her throat. Instead she closed her eyes for a moment and rubbed her temples to ease the beginnings of a headache that lurked there.

"You're tired." Gabe's voice seeped into the heavy fog she was drifting into. "Why don't you split and I'll hold the fort a little while longer?"

God knew how much she wanted to let him take over, but too often lately she had given into the urge to let Gabe protect her from her own fears. Her green eyes flickered open and she smiled at him.

"You go," she said finally. "I think Eileen and that little girl of yours might like to see you before midnight for a change. I told L.A. I'd be available here until ten o'clock, our time." She stifled a yawn. "I'll have some coffee, read a magazine. I'll be fine, Gabe."

He looked doubtful. "It's pretty late, Stef. Besides—" he leaned against her desk, his stubby fingers tapping against the wood—"aren't you heading up to Boston tomorrow morning to see your folks?"

She groaned. "My folks! Oh, God, I was supposed to call Mother this afternoon." She shook her head, then reached for the phone. "Go, Gabe." She waved her left hand toward the door. "Hell hath no fury like my mother uncalled. Spare yourself."

He laughed and picked up his suit jacket from the sofa on the other side of the small office. "If you need me, I'll have my beeper on all night."

She nodded her thanks as she dialed her parents' number.

"See you Tuesday!" With a wave of his hand Gabe slipped out the door. She could hear his heavy tread receding down the hallway toward the main lobby and the exit.

"Happy Labor Day!" she called out even though he couldn't hear her.

Her parents' line was busy so she placed the phone back on the console and paced her office, alternately bending and stretching to loosen her tension-tightened muscles. A coffeepot, eternally on, rested atop the narrow credenza beneath the window and she wandered over to pour herself a cup in an effort to keep awake.

As she rummaged around for a package of Sweet 'N Low in the wicker basket near the coffeemaker, she caught sight of a figure moving swiftly through the near-empty parking lot. She paused, coffee cup in hand, and watched the man jog easily across the asphalt toward a red Porsche parked at an angle beneath a street lamp.

Gabe running? Gabe Freeman believed running through the corridors of Conway News was exercise enough. Besides, he parked in the side lot near the security gatehouse and he could never afford a Porsche—not on his salary. She leaned closer to the window, narrowing her eyes as she watched the man brush drops of rain off his thick black curls—

Dan! Until he stepped beneath the circle of light, she had been unable to see the black outfit carelessly draped over one shoulder or the slightly wild yet well-cut black hair that framed his face.

She sipped her coffee, not noticing it was still unsweetened, while she watched him open the door to the sports car and, after shaking water off his shoulders, slide behind the wheel. The pool of light from the streetlamp slid down over the sleek car and illuminated the sharp, well-defined lines of his profile. Even from that distance, she could make out the straight nose, the shadow of his thick mustache, which topped a generous yet cleanly defined mouth, and the determined set of his taut jawline that even his beard couldn't hide. His headlights flashed on.

Somewhere in an apartment on Manhattan's East Side, a woman sipped Campari and soda and waited. Occasionally she would rise from the sofa to adjust the cool wail of jazz coming from the stereo or to make sure the candles on the intimate table à deux were at the right angle. She didn't have to check the blond hair that flowed like honey or the perfectly applied makeup that made her eyes glow like star sapphires. This woman had no insecurities: She knew she was what her man wanted.

Or maybe a woman and infant waited in a sprawling ranch house in Stony Brook or Cold Spring Harbor, their ears attuned for the sound of the red sports car in the driveway, the signal for that house to spring to life. The signal for that house to become a home.

The Porsche drove slowly around the parking lot and out the gate and Stefanie jumped as if ice water had been poured on her head.

"This is it," she said out loud. "I've finally gone over the edge. Looney Tunes time."

How long had she stood there weaving her bit of romantic fiction about a man she didn't even know? Why wasn't she congratulating herself for pulling Tele-Com out of the fire?

She knew the answer as well as she knew her own name, but she usually refused to dwell on it. Once upon a time she had envisioned a future that was nothing like the present in which she lived. In her teens and early twenties she had assumed with the naiveté of the very young—and the very romantic—that the right man would come along and sweep her up and away from the real world. She had gone along with her parents' ideas for her future because at heart she was an appeaser, and she had a definite talent for computer engineering. In her soul, however, she never believed that was all life would offer her. She had assumed that by twenty-eight she would have 2.3 children and be living in the suburbs. Well, she lived in the suburbs, and she was definitely twenty-eight, but the husband and children were as out of reach as ever.

If push came to shove, she would choose the life of the woman in the ranch house any day.

Stefanie crossed back to the desk, sat down, then leaned back in the padded leather swivel chair, resting her feet on top of a partially open lower desk drawer. The latest edition of *Connektions* magazine waited on the desk next to a pile of unanswered letters. *Connektions* was a great way to catch up on the latest happenings in the Long Island business community but lately she hadn't had the time to do the reading she should.

Now the office was empty, the phone was still, and she sat back to enjoy an article about a successful marketing executive who managed to juggle not only a demanding marriage to a doctor but also the very real problems involved in being mother to three active boys. It was an engrossing article, yet a part of her mind remained separate.

It was the silence.

Even as she read, she became aware of the deep, throbbing silence in the office. The apprehension that had tingled along her spine earlier had now spread its way up along her shoulders, making her scalp prickle. Except for the security guard at the main gate she was probably the only person left inside the huge industrial complex.

She tried to concentrate but the words snake-danced before her eyes and she was forced to put the magazine down while she rubbed her temples with slightly shaky fingers.

Just a few months ago this wouldn't have bothered her. Was it only last spring when she had been blissfully self-confident in her ability to handle herself? And, as it turned out, was it only last spring when she had also been totally ignorant as to just how dangerous a world it really was?

She could still remember the shock of metal pressed against her backbone, of rough words and rougher actions.

She pressed her hands over her eyes as if that action could blot out the memories of helplessness, of vulnerability. From that night on, her boundaries had begun their inexorable shrinking inward. The demands of her job became harder and harder to meet. Her position as liaison between Tele-Com and Conway demanded self-confidence and easy mobility— attributes she was no longer certain she possessed.

In two months she was expected to fly to Hawaii as part of Tele-Com's introduction of services to Conway's new overseas units. How was she going to manage a six-thousand-mile trip when the thought of the deserted parking lot right outside her office window made her heart thump wildly against her breastbone?

She looked at her slim tank watch and sighed. *It's ten P.M. Do you know where your executives are?* She laughed grimly. Time to go.

She stood up and stretched her arms high overhead, tucking the pale yellow silk blouse inside the waistband of her skirt. Without a backward glance at the window that looked out on her fears, she picked up her pocketbook and briefcase, plucked her suit jacket from the hook behind her door, then locked the office behind her.

With a step she prayed sounded more self-assured than she felt, she strode down the hallway and toward the exit to head for home.

2

"Mother, I said I'll bring the portfolio and I will."
Stefanie's voice was taut with frustration as she paced
the small kitchen of her apartment early the next
morning. Why on earth hadn't she remembered to try
her mother again last night? A lecture was one thing
she didn't need.

"Really, Stefanie, you haven't been yourself in quite
a while. Twenty-eight is a bit young for bouts of se-
nility, my girl."

Count to ten before you speak, Stephanie thought
as she drew in a deep breath and glanced out the window at the fine rain that misted her view of the woods
behind her apartment building. All in all, it was a rot-
ten start for the holiday weekend. She tried again.

"Mother, I didn't forget the portfolio last time. If
you recall, I had just driven down from Toronto and
I wasn't about to drive all the way home to get it." She
deliberately stretched out her words to exaggerate the
distance she would have to drive. Subtlety was usually lost on members of the Colt family.

"I don't think I care for your tone of voice, Stefanie." Elisabeth's voice had taken on the Boston-lady-lawyer tone that struck fear into district attorneys in three counties. "I am simply reminding you to bring the portfolio in order to save you the embarrassment of forgetting it. You know your brother is anxious to see those papers on the Tele-Com stock you recommended."

Balancing the phone between shoulder and ear, Stefanie poured herself a glass of orange juice and closed the refrigerator door with her hip.

"I'm not a stockbroker, Mother. I hope Brendan understands that. I'm merely passing along the information Gabe Freeman collected. That's all."

"Well, if you had arrived last night the way you'd planned, you could have told him yourself." There was a slight sigh from Elisabeth, and her daughter could hear it echo all the way from Massachusetts to New York. "Brendan's gone to see that young woman with the beach house on the Cape. He won't be back until Tuesday."

Stefanie's suppressed laugh made swallowing her orange juice difficult. "Her name is Katie, Mother."

"Indeed." Elisabeth's voice could freeze ice in Alaska.

Katie Keller was a very successful graphics artist who freelanced from her home on Cape Cod, a way of life the Colt family viewed with suspicion.

However, the last thing Stefanie wanted to get involved in at 7:00 A.M. was a discussion on life-styles. She willed her voice to stay even and pleasant.

"Mother, listen. I have a reservation on the nine o'clock ferry. I really should get going. It's an hour and a half drive to Orient Point and I have to allow for traffic, so—"

Her mother switched gears with the practiced ease of a trial lawyer. It was easy to see why the woman had become so successful. "You know, my dear, if you'd planned your time more precisely, you could have taken a flight up and saved yourself all this aggravation."

Stefanie's fingers tightened around the receiver.

"There is no aggravation, Mother, but there will be if I miss that ferry. This is Labor Day weekend and I was lucky to get that reservation as it is. Now, if I don't leave within the next forty-five seconds, I'll end up not coming at all."

"You know your father's pilot would have been happy to bring you up in the company jet if you'd—"

The fuse was lit and the explosion was imminent.

"Mother, I really must go. See you around one."

Before Elisabeth could manage another word, Stefanie had carefully replaced the phone in its wall cradle, marveling that she had resisted the urge to slam it down. Her mother's imperious ways were difficult enough to take; however, operating on as little sleep as Stefanie was—well, today just the sound of Elisabeth's dry, clipped voice was enough to send her daughter over the edge. Managing to seem as competent and dynamic as the rest of the clan was going to take every ounce of strength and courage Stefanie possessed. She'd been in a race with the rest of them, it seemed, since the day she was born.

She closed the red-and-white kitchen curtains and headed into the hallway to grab her leather purse, her briefcase, and her overnight bag. Her eyes traveled briefly around the living room. She noted the elegant lines of the charcoal-gray sofa, the sheen of the parquet floor, the understated sophistication of the Oriental carpet in the dining area. The entire room was in perfect balance, a hymn to harmony of design. TeleCom had provided the expensively decorated apartment for Stefanie when she took over sole control of the Conway account and needed daily access to Conway's corporate headquarters on Long Island. It was understated and sophisticated—so dignified that even her mother had approved. Yet to Stefanie it was strangely sterile. She had lived there for two years now and still had the feeling of just passing through, as if she were simply a transient on her way to somewhere else.

And the strangest thing of all, she thought as she closed the door behind her and crossed the wet lawn to the parking lot, was that she had felt that way all her life.

It's just that awful conversation with Mother, she told herself as she tossed her luggage into the trunk of the small Toyota then slammed the lid shut. Talking to Elisabeth always managed to leave her feeling agitated, more like a bumbling, backward child than a woman with a successful career.

She and her twin brother Brendan had been the unexpected "dividends" of Elisabeth's forty-first year. Elisabeth and her husband, Harrison Colt II, had thought their family completed—perfectly—eleven

years earlier after the births of their sons Harrison III
and Walker, both now successful attorneys.

Red-haired and high-tempered, the two infants were
unlike anyone else in the house—anyone else in the
family for the matter. They were obviously throw-
backs to some passionate Irishman in their mother's
lineage who was better left at peace. During his teens
and early adulthood Brendan had been hell-bent on
stirring up as much trouble in the Colt household as
humanly possible. Yet, despite that, he had managed
to get himself through law school and was now coun-
selor for a large publishing firm in Boston where he
had met Katie Keller.

Stefanie got into the car and started the engine,
gunning it more than necessary. Every holiday,
whether national, local, or personal—and most Sundays—she found herself on her way to Boston. Only
when she'd been in Europe or South America on
business was she excused from these formal family
gatherings. Even then, Stefanie mused as she steered
the car around a pothole the size of a small canal, the
unspoken message was "Jet planes do manage to zip
back and forth with ease."

She hated going and yet couldn't cope with the
possibility of saying no. Where Brendan needed no
one's approval but his own, Stefanie wanted love from
everyone, most especially from her mother. And visible love was the hardest thing for Elisabeth Colt to
show.

Her driving was slow, slightly erratic, as she made
her way to Orient Point for the ferry. As it turned out,
she barely had time to park in the small car line, race

through the drizzle to the offices near the snack bar to pick up her ticket, then hurry back across the sandy parking lot to get into her Toyota and follow the young attendant's loading instructions.

The attendant directed her to a spot on the right side of the ferry, next to the wall, and Stefanie breathed a sigh of relief that her car wouldn't be subjected to the damaging sea breezes that were capable of cutting right through layers of paint. Before she even had a chance to shut off her engine, the attendant had directed a green Pinto to park next to her and she had to squeeze her body gingerly through the tiny space her open door allowed. Weaving her way through the parked cars, she stepped outside onto the deck and climbed the slick metal stairs to the waiting room on port side to pick up a container of coffee.

A blue curtain of cigarette smoke hung over the air downstairs and loud rumbles of conversation filled the small waiting room. People were crowded hip-to-hip on the metal benches, juggling hot chocolate and *Newsday* on their laps while children raced up and down the length of the room crying, "When will we be there, Mommy?" A few hardier souls, smoking cigarettes and chatting idly, settled on the floor beneath the window. There was an air of camaraderie that only a three-day weekend in New York can produce.

She could hardly wait to pay for her coffee and get out of there.

Even though it was chilly outside and the rain somehow managed to seep through her yellow terry-cloth sweat shirt, she preferred the isolation of the top deck. Stefanie loved watching the ferry cut its own pattern through the choppy gray-green waters as it glided toward Connecticut.

She leaned forward and rested her elbows on the railing and let her mind drift lazily around like the seagull who dipped and soared overhead. No ringing phones, no irate customers, no family obligations. For a little over an hour she could disappear.

Most of her life she had spent making herself available to other people, and lately, although she was loathe to admit it, she was beginning to tire of the role. She was nearly twenty-nine years old and she still felt not entirely in control of her own future.

She chuckled out loud. Maybe her mother was right. Maybe she was becoming senile. . . .

"Private joke?"

Stefanie jumped at the sound of the male voice and the touch of the hand on her shoulder and knocked the container of coffee over the railing and into the Long Island Sound.

For a split second her mind went blank with the unreasonable fear that surfaced time after time. Then she found herself looking into the same pair of merry eyes, impossibly starred with bristly black lashes, that had captivated her the night before. The eyes were blue. Very blue.

"It *is* Stefanie, isn't it?"

"That's right," she answered, extending her right hand in greeting. "Stefanie Colt. You're Dan—"

"O'Connor," he supplied, clasping her hand with his. Was it his imagination or had he seen more than a normal look of surprise when she spun around to face him? "Actually, the whole name is Daniel Patrick O'Connor, but no one believes a *sensei* could have a name like that.''

Her forehead wrinkled. *''Sen-sigh?''*

''Teacher.'' She looked up at him with the strangest eyes he'd ever seen. Large and heavy-lidded, they managed to convey intelligence, sexiness, and vulnerability simultaneously. He wished the sun were out, wished he could step closer to her to see if they were simply hazel or the cool dark green of a forest. ''I run training courses in self-defense for different corporations in the metro area. I was giving the last part of a seminar yesterday when I saw you at Conway.''

''So that was it,'' she said with an easy laugh. She was in control once again, fears securely pushed aside. ''I thought I'd stumbled onto a location for a kung fu movie.''

''Please,'' he said with a groan. ''Don't even mention me in the same breath with that garbage. I spent God-knows-how-many years out in Hollywood teaching muscle-brained jocks how to look macho for the camera. I'm still trying to live it down.''

''They were that bad?''

He grinned at her. ''The movies or the actors?''

His grin was slightly lopsided; it tilted up more on the left side than the right. She couldn't decide what was more attractive: the way his mustache twitched with his words or the even row of large white teeth that flashed dangerous and bright against his dark, closely-trimmed beard.

''What made you turn your back on the klieg lights and glamor of Tinsel Town?''

There was a hesitation. His handsome face seemed to close in upon itself for a moment. She watched, fascinated, as his thoughts whirled visibly across his deep blue eyes.

"Trends change," he answered finally with a shrug. "Bruce Lee died, *Saturday Night Fever* was born, the public's interest switched to dance movies."

"And you can't dance?" Her voice acknowledged that he, too, had his secrets.

He met her look with appreciation. "And I can't dance."

A violent gust of wind blew up off the water, making them move closer together instinctively.

"Feels more like November than September, doesn't it?" Stefanie said. She turned toward Dan, who was leaning over the railing, supporting his weight on his elbows. The wind blew his dark smoky curls across his forehead and she felt the desire to stroke them gently back and feel their softness against her skin. "It's been so cold," she said instead.

"The weather's been changing the past few years," he said, turning toward her. "Winters seem to be getting milder and summers colder."

"But we had a blizzard this year." She was growing mesmerized by the darkness of his eyes. "I'd hardly call that a mild winter."

"You can't judge by that," he said, not swayed by her logic. "Blizzards are freak occurrences. If you examine the last ten or fifteen years, there seems to be a definite switch in our weather patterns."

Her voice was light with laughter. "You're not one of those who think men on the moon changed our weather patterns, are you?"

He turned his megawatt grin on her full force. "I can't think of a better explanation, can you?"

"The shifting of glaciers, nuclear testing, the thinning of our ozone layer, the greenhouse effect...."

"Enough!" His face registered comical outrage. "Where's the romance in your soul, Stefanie Colt?"

She said something but her words didn't penetrate the spell he found himself falling under. Another gust of wind blew her auburn hair across her face and Dan suddenly felt like sheltering her within the circle of his arms. Protecting her. The faint circles beneath her eyes and the paleness of her lightly freckled skin made her seem younger than she had the night before. He kept seeing that brief flash of fear on her face and he wanted to be the one to erase it.

He wasn't listening to her. How could she blame him? She had never been so dull, so totally boring in her entire life. "Laverne and Shirley" would sound like Shakespeare compared to the drivel she'd been spouting. He watched her lips the way a deaf man would, as if trying to glean meaning from movement, and she found herself beginning to stammer the way she used to at the dinner table when her parents made her practice her French.

"Are you always so rude?" Her words were sharp, in direct contrast to the natural sweetness of her voice.

He reddened beneath his tan. "No, not always," he said with a self-deprecating laugh. "My brain doesn't switch into gear until noon." He picked up her left wrist and glanced at her watch. "I'm not legally responsible for my stupidity for another two and a half hours." He leaned nearer to her. "Now, what did you say before?"

A smile passed across her face like quicksilver slipping through a magician's hand.

"Are you a regular on the ferry?" she repeated. "I don't remember seeing you here before. I'm sure I would have noticed you." Damn! What a stupid, stupid thing to say. *Whatever happened to playing your cards close to your vest, Colt?*

"My maiden voyage," he said. "I used to take I-95, but when the Mianus River Bridge collapsed—" he shook his head, thinking of the disaster that had claimed lives a while back "—well, I decided this was a hell of a lot safer."

He fixed the collar on his short leather bomber jacket, smoothing it over the way he had smoothed over her embarrassment. A part of him had noticed her slip and savored it. She felt the same awareness, the same possibilities as he did. He was sure of it now.

"Where are you headed, if I might ask?" Her voice was cool and pleasant, the Queen of England asking him to tea.

"Newport. I'm going to spend the weekend playing first mate on a sailboat." He turned his electric grin on her. "Why don't you come along? Jim and Maureen love company and the boat sleeps six."

"Sounds marvelous." She could be as casual as he. "However, I'm expected at the familial dinner table by one P.M."

"Do you always do what's expected?"

"Usually. I find life is simpler that way."

Dan tilted his head closer to hers until she could smell the clean scent of his hair. "Come with me," he said, his grin softening into a slightly unsure smile. "We could make some very delightful complications."

His invitation had popped out the way his words usually did: glib, facile, unplanned. He hadn't realized how much he wanted her to say yes until she refused.

"My life is complicated enough," she answered, her voice still maddeningly even. "One thing I don't need is having to explain to my mother why I suddenly opted to spend the weekend on a boat with total strangers. It might be too much for her."

"Are you certain it wouldn't be too much for you?"

Her eyes darkened to a dangerous shade of green. "You flatter yourself, *Sensei.*"

Somehow they had stumbled quickly, unwittingly, to within a heartbeat of one another's individual boundaries, and with the well-developed instincts of very private people, they retreated into silence. In a second she had found herself hating him for asking her to come away with him, then hating herself for being too cowardly, too cautious, to take him up on it. He made her feel as out of her depth as if she had plunged into the chilly sound that rushed past the ferry. With Dan she would be too far from shore.

Next to her he cleared his throat.

"You were drinking coffee when I startled you," he said, the sound of New England more evident when he was unsure of himself. "Why don't I go down and get you another cup before they close the snack bar?"

"You don't have to do that," she answered. "Their coffee is best suited to being tossed overboard anyway."

"I insist." He touched her shoulder. "I'll be right back. Wait here."

Stefanie watched as he walked away and disappeared below deck, his full head of glossy curls the last thing to drop from view. She turned back to the railing and yanked at the zipper on her yellow sweat shirt, pulling it up close around her throat. Why hadn't she realized how cold and damp it was on deck? Perhaps when Dan was there, his muscular body had shielded her from the wind, kept the cold from seeping into her bones.

Dangerous, she thought. Very dangerous. She could learn to like that feeling very easily.

She stared moodily at the approaching Connecticut shoreline, which was dotted with beautiful estates and mansions that loomed elegant and self-contained in the distance. Hundreds of small sailboats with sails of white and yellow and red and blue fluttered in the wind, choking the waters in a beautiful maritime traffic jam. Now and then a few souls, dressed in jackets and long pants, would whistle to the ferry from their sailboats and wave, arms describing exaggerated arcs in the chilled September air.

You're a fool, Colt, she thought. This is how it's done: Handsome man meets reasonably attractive woman. He has an hour to kill. How better to spend his time than exercising his charm, flexing it the way some men flex their biceps? Great practice for the real thing. No promises. No truths. Just fun, plain and simple.

No other adult woman would have taken his flirtatious invitation seriously. It was no wonder his mind had started to wander while they talked. She glanced around the deck at the people hurrying down to start their cars for disembarkation. The ferry was already backing into the slip and he hadn't returned.

He wasn't going to return.

Another lesson: Brush-off 101.

She grabbed her car keys from her pocket and headed down to the vehicle deck.

The snack bar was closing as he approached it and it took every ounce of persuasive charm he had at his command—not to mention a five-dollar bill—to persuade the gray-haired woman behind the counter to give him a cup of coffee. He waved off cream and sugar and, grabbing a lid, raced out of the lounge, swearing loudly when drops of hot coffee burned the inside of his wrist.

He took the iron steps two at a time up to the top deck. The ferry was being secured to the slip and passengers were already squeezing their ways into their cars in preparation for departure.

She was nowhere. The deck was tiny—there was no way he could miss her.

A man in a plaid sport coat headed toward the stairs and Dan, oblivious to his usual respect for body space, grabbed his arm.

"Excuse me," he said, his voice more harried than normal, "did you see an attractive red-haired woman up here?"

The man looked up at him, his watery blue eyes blank.

"She's about an inch or two shorter than you, yellow sweater..."

The man still stared at Dan, eyes vacant.

"Two front teeth missing, green feathers in her ears?"

The plaid sport coat hurried away.

"Damn!" Dan tossed the liquid overboard and stuffed the empty cup into a trash container.

It was no wonder she'd taken the first chance to slip away. He'd been a fool—a complete fool—to ask her to spend the weekend with him, even if Jim and Maureen were going to be there, too. This wasn't some sleazy singles bar and he was light-years past that scene.

Stefanie was meant for candlelight and champagne and a slow, careful wooing.

There had been lulls, those awkward silences that punctuate the conversation of virtual strangers, but he had thought she felt the same unspoken attraction he had.

He combed his fingers through the thick mop of curls that were beginning to show a few random strands of silver.

"You blew it," he said out loud as he turned to go below deck to get his car. He knew her name and where she worked. It wouldn't be hard to contact her.

But he was a proud man. She had made her choice and he'd honor it.

Even if regret burned right through his heart.

The pain beneath her ribs, her ulcer's persistent reminder, burned hotter as she waited her turn to drive off the ferry. Exhaust fumes, acrid and choking, filled her lungs as she watched the young attendant try to unload the ferry quickly and safely.

"Yo! Over there! Silver Toyota."

She looked up at the tall skinny man who stood twenty feet away. He motioned her forward and to the right, then had her wait while three Volkswagens and a Chevette inched down the ramp.

When her turn came she had to maneuver past an elderly couple in a cream-colored Mercedes convertible and she held her breath until she had driven safely off.

The drizzly, pale gray skies suited both her mood and the drabness of the dockside. Cars snaked single file past a string of Amtrak railroad cars to the traffic light where the highway intersected the access road. Her mind skittered around like the raindrops on her windshield. It refused to remain focused on her slow progress in the line of traffic. It refused to concentrate on the family weekend ahead. It stubbornly refused to zero in on anything but Dan O'Connor.

Her eyes darted to her rearview mirror, repeatedly searching the stream of cars and trucks behind her. She wouldn't admit it, but she was trying to catch a glimpse of a flashy red Porsche and a dazzling grin.

If she'd been paying attention, she might have seen the black Mazda ride up along the right shoulder and cut in front of her.

But she hadn't been paying attention, so her first indication of trouble was the metallic crunch of fender against fender.

Stefanie pushed hard on the brake, but before she could even throw the car into neutral and turn off the ignition, the driver of the Mazda ejected himself from behind the steering wheel with the speed of a pilot abandoning a flaming plane, and was storming toward her, fists clenched, ready to do battle.

3

"Hey, man! What the hell kind of driver are you?" The man's words echoed all around her.

"I could ask the same of you," Stefanie said, temper simmering, ready to boil. She unsnapped her seat belt and got out. The other driver, husky and blond, stood where the two cars were obscenely joined. The veins in his neck throbbed with fury.

She bent down and touched her hand to the spot where hers was damaged.

"Did you have to push your way in?" She stood and faced the husky man who loomed beside her. "Haven't you ever heard of waiting your turn?"

"You women shouldn't be allowed on the road," he said, moving closer.

His breath was warm and yeasty and a cloud of beer seemed to hover over him. The smell, especially so early in the morning, made her feel ill. She tried to step back but the backs of her knees were pressed against the crumpled bumper.

"Can't drive worth a damn," he went on. "Should never have let you out of the kitchen." He took his time, letting his eyes trail up her body from the long slim legs, around the curved hips, over her breasts to her face. "In your case, out of the bedroom."

He was large but he wasn't massive. She straightened her spine and met his eyes, praying her fear wouldn't show.

"If you'll move, I'd like to go across the road and call the police. We'll have to exchange licenses, insurance info—"

"Why don't we exchange phone numbers instead?" A heavy hand clamped down on her shoulder. The sour smell of beer made Stefanie's stomach lurch. "We don't have to bring the cops into this. Who needs to have their premiums raised, right?" The grip on her shoulder tightened. "Two adults can find a way to work it out, hmm?"

That was the way it always happened: aggression and sexuality battling for dominance. She'd seen it happen before, been poised on the knife's edge, not knowing which threat held the greater danger. That other time she had felt the anger and touch of lust meld into a dangerous combination that sought out the first victim. Her mind began to freeze over in a set pattern of fear. She was going under....

"Come on," the man urged. "We'll find someplace to have a drink and talk about it—"

"You'll have to talk about it with the cops, pal. They're on their way."

It was Dan, his voice calm and even as he took control of the situation. He had seen her, arms wrapped protectively around her chest, manage to get herself backed against her car. He glanced over at her, noting the hunted look in her deep green eyes. Make no mistake about it, he would find out what caused that look. But first this problem had to be attended to.

"This is a private matter, man." The light-haired man eyed Dan then dismissed him as no trouble. "The little lady and I can work things out fine."

Dan turned to Stefanie. "Is that true?"

She shook her head. Waves of relief had silenced her voice.

He turned back to the owner of the Mazda.

"Why don't you get your insurance card and registration out and we'll get things moving?"

"Why don't you get yourself out of here by getting yourself moving?" The man's voice had risen in anger.

A crowd had gathered and Stefanie's ears picked up on the buzz of anticipation and apprehension.

It happened so quickly that afterward she had to replay the scene in her mind to understand what had really occurred. The blond man had followed up on his words with a sudden punch. In a split second Dan, cool and outwardly calm, positioned himself between Stefanie and the aggressor, his left forearm blocking the blow. Then he easily grabbed the other man's wrist and slowly, almost casually, turned it until the bigger man sank to his knees, anger turning to surprise.

The sound of the policeman's voice brought Stefanie back to reality.

"What's the problem, folks?"

She turned toward the policeman, then cast a swift glance at Dan and then at the other man, who was crouching near the hood of his car rubbing his wrist.

"Just a fenderbender, officer," she said, finally turning back to him. "We seem to have everything under control."

It was after eleven in the morning when all the paperwork was finally completed and the other driver had been hauled in for driving under the influence of alcohol. Stefanie had thanked Dan for all his help and found her thanks pushed aside when he insisted she come for breakfast with him.

She demurred at first, claiming a long drive still ahead of her, but faced with the sheer force of his magnetism, she finally gave in and followed him to a small restaurant a few miles away.

"Thanks, Dan," she said ten minutes later as she sipped coffee from a white china mug and sank back against the padded seat. "You were right. I really needed this." He had been more right than even she had first realized. The aftermath of her brush with random violence had left her feeling shaky and vulnerable.

"When I promise a lady a cup of coffee, I deliver," Dan said, digging into a plate of pancakes and sausages dripping with Vermont maple syrup.

She laughed and gestured toward her own plate, which overflowed with scrambled eggs, Canadian bacon, and toast.

"You delivered more than you promised."

He lowered his fork and looked directly into her eyes. "I usually do."

There were no shades of meaning in his remarks, no sly innuendo. It was a sexual statement, blatant and powerful.

She found it impossible to break his midnight gaze, but equally impossible to allow it to continue. It couldn't continue.

She cleared her throat by taking another sip of coffee.

"I appreciate your help back there," she said, wishing he wouldn't watch her face quite so closely. "I don't know how it got so scary so quickly."

"Don't you?"

She frowned. "No, I don't. Do you?"

He leaned across the small table. "You allowed it to happen."

She put her cup down with a loud bang. "You're insane!" He didn't flinch at her outburst. She crossed her arms over her chest and glared at him. "Tell me how I allowed it to happen."

He ticked off the list of "transgressions" on long tanned fingers.

"You let him get too close; you assumed a vulnerable position"—he pointed to her arms-across-chest pose—"just like that; you bent down in front of him, letting him take a shot at you if he wanted; and you didn't maintain firm eye contact."

At his words her arms had dropped to her sides, where they dangled awkwardly against her body.

"Eye contact?" She laughed. "He was too busy seeing double to notice."

Dan leaned back in his seat.

"Exactly. You were sober; he wasn't. You had all the advantages and you didn't use a one."

"Being backed against a car hardly constitutes an advantage in my book."

That dynamite grin of his exploded once again.

"That's my point. You never should have allowed that to happen."

"Damn it!" Her hand slapped the table in frustration. "Hasn't anyone ever told you people don't choose to be victims?" His unwitting criticisms had brought her to instant fury. "It just happens."

"Like hell it does." His voice matched hers in passion. "You should have been keeping a space between you and him. You should have maneuvered yourself sideways to look at the damage to your car. You had options."

Harsh words. They found their mark.

"You have all the answers, don't you?" Stefanie's voice was sharp, her words staccato. "I suppose I should get myself a cute little pair of white pajamas and learn to break boards with my feet?"

"If it turns you on." His voice was harder, more controlled than before. "It won't do a damn thing for you on the street, though."

"And, of course, you know what will?"

He leaned forward, long fingers tapping against his coffee cup.

"It's my business to know."

Her eyes darted around the small restaurant, lingering for one long moment on a family across the room, on the pale curls of the baby in the high chair. She forced her eyes back to meet Dan's.

"Is it also your business," she asked, her voice quieter now, "to know how to stop feeling scared? How to force your brain to work when you feel frozen inside, when you're too frightened to move, too scared to stay?"

He was right. She had been hurt, had been one of the yearly total of victims. A statistic. But, as his brother Michael had been, she was flesh and blood and feelings, something no statistic ever conveyed.

He reached across the table and touched her hand briefly.

"Yes," he answered. "I know how to change those things, Stefanie. I could make a difference." He spoke on two levels but would be pleased if she only heard him on the obvious one. For now.

Her anger cooled down as abruptly as it had flared up. She directed her attention to the eggs in front of her, which looked greasy and unpleasant. She had told him more in the last exchange than she had told anyone about what had happened to her. He kept managing to zero right in on her insecurities, peeling them away layer by layer until she feared raw nerve would be exposed.

They ate in silence. Although she avoided looking directly at him, she found herself aware of the fast movement of his fork. Two times he had called the waitress over to refill his coffee, to bring him more jam for his toast. Vibrations of pure sensual enjoyment radiated outward from him, almost touching her. Warming her.

Stefanie cut a piece of bacon with the side of her fork, then brought it to her mouth, trying hard not to notice the congealed fat around the edges.

"Put your fork down."

"I beg your pardon?" Her fork was poised an inch from her mouth.

"That looks as appetizing to you as rattlesnake meat. Order something else."

She hesitated, thinking of an icy wedge of canteloupe and a croissant, but good manners, dominant after twenty-eight years, won out.

"No, thank you. This is just fine." She popped the bacon in to her mouth, chewed the greasy mess twice, then swallowed it. "See? Absolutely marvelous."

He looked at her, noted the spark of gold reborn in her dark green eyes, and he laughed. Without preamble, he slid her plate across the Formica table to his side.

"Listen, I can be a pushy son of a bitch sometimes." He laughed again. "Old habits die hard. I ordered for both of us before you had a chance to come out of the ladies' room."

The look he gave her melted her reserve.

"Give my guilty conscience a break and order something you like." Those midnight-blue eyes of his centered on her, focused, then drew her inside. "Please?"

"I hate to see food go to waste . . ." she began, gesturing toward her plate.

"It won't." He stabbed a piece of Canadian bacon with his fork and started to eat.

Her laugh was a burst of delightful sound—loud, surprisingly uninhibited, completely unexpected. To Dan it was like the sound of a cooling shower on a hot day. He called the waitress over.

Minutes later Stefanie was savoring the cool explosion of canteloupe against her tongue.

She sighed. "Marvelous. Just perfect."

Dan had just demolished two breakfasts and looked askance at the slender wedge of melon and the flaky croissant in front of her.

"That's it?" He sounded incredulous. "That's not enough to feed a parakeet." He glanced around again for the waitress. "That'll never hold you till dinner."

She finished buttering the croissant and smiled at him.

"Less than this usually holds me till dinner."

His thick black eyebrows slashed down toward his nose and his eyes seemed to darken.

"Impossible." He raised his arm to signal to the waitress, who was stacking glasses on a tray on the other side of the restaurant.

"No, Dan. Please." On impulse, her hand darted across the table and grasped his forearm. The long muscles lay coiled tight and hard beneath her fingertips. Her index finger rested atop a vein and she registered the strong and steady pulse within.

At her touch, he met her eyes and she had the sensation of being drawn into him, body and soul, pulled closer to his heart.

Quite an imagination you have, Colt, she thought.

"I usually have just a cup of coffee," she continued, her voice sounding softer than before, more yielding. "On a good day, I have a Milky Way bar with it."

She smiled and his eyes drifted to her mouth. Her bright peach lipstick had faded, giving her a more delicate look, emphasizing the sweet fullness of her lips. She would taste sweet, Dan thought. He needed to know how sweet. He changed the subject.

"How do you manage to look so healthy?"

She grinned. "Good genes, I guess."

His look was one of frank appreciation. "Remind me to send a check to the American Genetic Research Foundation."

"Anything for a tax deduction." Her words were flip, but the slight glow on her cheeks told him his meaning had been clear.

She was startled when he closed his hand over hers, pressing her palm against his warm flesh. His gaze swept over the curve of her narrow pointed chin, slid over the prominent cheekbones that reminded him of a young Katharine Hepburn, then sought her moss green eyes.

"Look at me, Stefanie." *See me.*

She knew if she looked up he would see what she was feeling, feel the unmistakable flare of electricity sparking from every fiber.

"Stefanie?"

It was inevitable as his heartbeat. She lifted her eyes and he felt a pain barrel through him with the force of a cannonball, causing his breathing to become shallow, something no longer reflexive but a thing requiring thought and effort.

So this was how it felt. He'd always wondered about it, but had doubted he'd ever be lucky enough to find out.

"Spend the weekend with me."

Stefanie's hand moved back from his.

"I know it sounds crazy, but don't pull away." His voice was husky, yet the rougher edges were smoothed over by desire.

Dan's fingers curled around her hand and she couldn't stop her own fingers from clasping his in response. His eyes held her in thrall and she was powerless to break the spell that had suddenly—magically—surrounded them.

But she must.

"Dan . . . I can't."

"Why not?"

"I hardly know you."

His laugh was low and appealingly uncertain.

"After this weekend you would."

She shook her head and withdrew her hand from his, almost disappointed he didn't resist.

"I'll tell you everything you need to know about me: I'm thirty-four; I'm clean, healthy, brave, and true. I'm a self-defense specialist; I like Michael Jackson's music, Al Pacino's movies, Irish whiskey, and Italian food." He turned his hands palm up. "Did I forget anything?"

She spoke without thinking. "Are you married?"

The devilish gleam in his eyes glittered bright.

"Do you think I'd be here with you if I were?"

Her narrow shoulders lifted in a shrug.

"People aren't always what they seem to be."

A dull ache started deep inside his chest. He hadn't allowed himself to think that she might be married. He forced himself not to glance at her left hand.

"Are you what you seem?"

Her laugh was high and slightly jittery.

"If I seem to be a twenty-eight-year-old woman with a sharp temper and a nervous stomach, then I am."

He waited, his breathing suspended for the moment.

"Married?"

She met his eyes. "Afraid not."

Relief rushed through him like white water in the rapids.

"Were you ever married?" Now that he knew her present, he needed to know her past.

She frowned slightly, causing small furrows to appear on her forehead.

"If we're playing Twenty Questions, when do I get my turn?" Her voice grew a shade cooler.

A red flush stained Dan's neck, visible even through his tan.

"Sorry. That was none of my business, was it?"

"No, it wasn't." She had overreacted so she softened her words with a gentle smile. "But the answer is no. I've never been married." She needed to answer him.

He was totally attuned to her now, could feel a shadow of sadness fall across her.

"You have something against the institution?" He was trying to keep his tone light, but his need for answers tore through the sheer fabric of his facade.

"No, I don't have anything against the institution. It's just that if I'm going to be institutionalized, I want to make darn sure I approve of my fellow inmate."

They laughed and she was sure she'd defused the growing seriousness of their conversation. He was relentless, however, in his need to know all.

"Any close calls?"

Stefanie shook her head and a thick wave of coppery hair fell across her left eye. He reached over the table and lifted it away from her skin, relishing the cool silky feel of it against his flesh.

"You're lovely," he breathed. "I find it hard to believe that you're unattached."

She was finding it hard to think with his hand so near to touching her cheekbone. "I'm not a casual woman," she managed finally. "I never learned how to manage casual relationships."

"I'm glad." His voice was a murmur. No longer could he resist the urge to touch the delicate peach of her cheek. He let his index finger slip along the curve of her face and trace the surprisingly strong outline of her jaw. "Casual relationships are highly overrated."

"So I've heard."

"Will that be all, folks?"

At the sound of the waitress's voice, Stefanie and Dan moved apart to opposite sides of the table like guilty children caught in the cookie jar.

Dan looked at her. "More coffee?"

She glanced down at her watch. "Oh, God! It's nearly noon." She reached over for her purse and car keys. "I'm supposed to be in Boston in an hour."

"Just the check, please," he said to the waitress, then turned to Stefanie. "Your family dinner?"

She groaned. "My family dinner."

He glanced at the check, tossed the tip down, then stood up.

"Maybe you should call them."

She shook her head as she stood up next to him, thinking about the unpleasant conversation she'd had with her mother earlier that morning.

"Why waste the time?" she answered as they walked toward the cashier's booth. "I could be in Rhode Island by the time I got off the phone."

He chuckled as he took his change from the cashier and held the door open for Stefanie.

Outside the rain had slowed to a chilly mist.

"I can't tell if it's cool for late summer or warm for early fall," he said as they half-ran through the parking lot toward their cars.

She looked up at the pale sky that was still streaked with rain clouds the color of steel.

"Not much of a summer this year, was it?" she said.

They stopped in front of her car. The switch to casual conversation had been abrupt and it left her feeling awkward. She fitted her key into the lock, turned it, and opened the door. She looked again at Dan, who stood leaning against his red Porsche, parked at an angle next to her silver Toyota.

"Well," she said, car keys jingling in her hand.

He grinned that marvelous lopsided grin of his and stepped closer to her.

"Well."

He took her car keys away and closed his fist around the metal that was warm from her flesh.

"Last chance to change your plans."

She held out her hand and he dropped the heavy key ring into her open palm.

"I'm afraid I don't dare risk my mother's fury."

He inclined his head toward her in a gesture of defeat as she got into her car and rolled down the window on the driver's side.

"Well, thank you again for all your help," she said as she started the engine. "I don't know what I would have done without you."

"I want to see you again, Stefanie."

"Dan, I—"

There it was again, that look of apprehension and uncertainty.

He pressed a finger to her lips.

"Dinner on Friday," he said. Then he drew his finger across her lips, gently trailing down her throat to the opening of her yellow jacket.

Her words were stuck somewhere deep in her chest. "Stefanie?"

"No—I mean, I usually work late on Friday." She was floundering and she knew it, torn between her strong desire to see him again and the need to stand back and take careful stock of what was happening between them.

Behind them a man leaned on his horn, motioning in a rather vulgar fashion that he was tired of waiting for the parking spot.

She glanced in her rearview mirror. "I think I'd better get moving," she said. "I've had enough trouble for one day."

"One minute." Dan reached into his back pocket, yanked out his wallet, and removed a business card, which he handed to her. "I teach a class for women in street safety on Tuesday and Thursday nights. I'd like you to come as my guest."

She hesitated. He pressed the card into her hand. "What can you lose?" he persisted. "Two hours of your time?"

He wanted her to see him where he felt most comfortable, most valuable. He clasped her hand.

"You'll come?"

She nodded, not really knowing if she would. His mouth seemed to be hovering near her and she had a mad desire to pull his face down to hers and kiss him.

"Will you move it somewhere else?" The man behind them was growing more impatient.

Dan moved away from the car.

"Drive carefully," he said as she backed out of the spot.

"I promise." She waved and pulled out of the lot.

His fingers held the touch of her long after her slightly damaged car disappeared around the curve.

So he hadn't imagined that fleeting look of fear that washed across her face and disappeared as quickly as it came. He'd worked too long with people who had suffered physical assaults not to recognize the signs. Since his brother, Michael, a former police officer, had been killed in a street attack, Dan had become acutely sensitive to exactly how prevalent crime was. He wouldn't rush her, wouldn't push her into a closeness she wasn't ready for.

But he had waited thirty-four years to find her and he wasn't about to let her go.

Connecticut slid into Rhode Island and Rhode Island was just a name on the map as Stefanie headed north to Boston.

She herself hovered in some timeless place, suspended in daydreams. Dan.

Nothing about him fit. Try as she might, she couldn't force the pieces of him into a tidy manageable shape. A rough, unruly edge always jutted out, ruining the harmony of the whole.

His accent was undeniably Boston, but different from hers. His was the sound of the streets, while hers was the sound of the silent banks and libraries. His face bore the marks of brawling and his eyes had the look of a man who'd seen the other side of life and been changed by it. She felt certain that his Porsche had been earned, dollar by dollar, and was appreciated by him in a way she could never fully understand.

She whizzed past the Welcome to Massachusetts sign and felt the burning sensation beneath her ribs flare into life. She laughed out loud as she imagined Elisabeth's face if Dan—bearded, leather-jacketed and decidedly Porsched—roared up the cobbled driveway to the staid Colt family home to explain why her daughter was late for dinner. Why, the Colt family thought it in questionable taste just to drive a sports car before sunset.

He was too much: too raw, too potently masculine, too secure in who and what he was. His power and strength were so much a part of him that his intensity was hypnotic. Looking into those dark, oddly blue eyes of his, she had found herself wanting to unburden herself to him, to absorb some of his strength and make it her own.

And yet a simple thing like giving him her home address had given her pause, made her withdraw when she longed to move forward. Her fears had already begun to narrow her work boundaries and now they tugged at her social boundaries as well.

She reached over and touched the business card that was tucked into the outer compartment of her purse.

Maybe.

4

"You're late, Stefanie." Elisabeth Colt, tall, willowy, and eternally tan, was clipping flowers in the garden when Stefanie came up the walk.

"Glad to see you too, Mother." Stefanie put her small overnight bag down on the flagstone path and lightly kissed her mother's cheek. She glanced at the wicker basket filled with orange marigolds and white impatiens and raised an eyebrow in question. "New hobby?"

Elisabeth peeled off a pair of stiff new garden gloves and tossed them on top of the flowers in the basket.

"The doctor thinks I should have an outlet for some of my tensions besides my law practice." She gestured toward the small garden that ran along the front of the house and around the western wall. "Brendan and Katie heard that and came over one Friday at the crack of dawn and planted this garden." She shook her head. "They were out here for eight hours—never once took a break. Amazing."

Stefanie shot her mother a glance as they strolled around the side of the house to the back door. "Also very generous, don't you think?"

Elisabeth's mouth crinkled as she pursed her lips. "When it comes to analyzing your brother's motives, well, I've ceased trying."

Stefanie held the screen door open with her hip for her mother, then followed her into the sunroom at the rear of the house. "Will they be here for dinner?" she asked after Elisabeth had given directions to the new housekeeper on arranging the flowers. She had to stifle a giggle. This was definitely not the hobby the doctor had in mind for Elisabeth.

"If the spirit moves them to be here. That's how they do things lately—on impulse." She glanced at her slim Cartier tank watch. "Fortunately not all of my children are guided by their impulses. Dinner will be at seven." Her dark gray eyes took in Stefanie's small suitcase. "Is that all you have with you or is your luggage in the car?"

"This is it, Mother. One thing my job has taught me is how to travel light."

Elisabeth led the way from the enclosed sunporch into the main portion of the house.

"Tele-Com still has you working at Conway News Service?" she asked, running her long fingers absently over the top of the rosewood buffet in the formal dining room where she had stopped to check the seating arrangements.

"Until the end of the year," Stefanie said, heading toward the hall staircase. Her mother, who had asked her the same question a week ago, was as unable to remember details about her daughter's life today as she had been twenty years ago. "My contract is up for renegotiation with Tele-Com in December." She shifted the suitcase to her left hand. "Are Harrison and Walker here yet?"

Elisabeth nodded, inspecting invisible dust on the buffet. "Harrison and Mary are out visiting friends and Walker and Madolyn are having luncheon with her aunt Miranda."

An enormous wave of fatigue swept over Stefanie and she stifled a yawn. "I'm going to lie down for a while before dinner, Mother. I had a long drive."

Elisabeth looked at her daughter for a second, a flicker of concern passing across her lean and handsome face. "Fine, dear," she said at last. "I really must do something about that new housekeeper."

Stefanie stood at the foot of the staircase and watched her mother reflexively straighten her shoulders, stiffen her spine, then walk out of the dining room. The same indomitable spirit that kept her working through illness and approaching old age was the same spirit that made it impossible for her to show affection.

I do love you, Mother, Stefanie thought as she slowly climbed the staircase to her old room on the second floor, *but sometimes I don't like you very much at all.*

"Beer?"

Dan opened his eyes and took the cold can from Jim. It was nearing dusk and everything had that ethereal blue haze of approaching evening.

"Thanks." He popped the top and took a long swig, savoring the feel of the foam buzzing against his lips as the beer slipped down his throat.

Jim, as blond as Dan was dark, sat alongside his brother-in-law and propped his feet up on the boat's railing.

"Feel like talking about it?"

Dan took another sip of beer, then put the can down on the deck next to the plate with the half-eaten ham on rye left over from lunch.

"There's nothing to talk about, Jimmy. I'm just enjoying the sea breezes." He grinned at his friend but his eyes stayed serious. "That's why you invite me out on this tub, isn't it?"

"Like hell it is." Jim's voice was teasing but he watched his friend closely. "Mo and I need an extra pair of hands."

"Come on, have a heart! I thought you took pity on me and invited me out for some rest."

Jim threw his hands in the air. "What are you—a charity case who drives a Porsche 944? We invite you out so you can remember how the other half lives."

Dan shot him a wry glance. "Where I came from the other half didn't have a forty-seven-foot sloop."

"This is Newport, pal," Jim said with his easy laugh. "We make our own rules."

Dan fell back into his contemplative mood. Jim sat awhile and watched his friend of seventeen years sit strangely silent, his midnight-blue eyes focused somewhere out on the horizon.

"Jimmy! Give me a hand with the steaks, will you?"

Mo's voice floated up from the galley and Jim went down to help his wife.

"What's up?" he asked, his eyes making a quick sweep of the galley area, which was immaculate and showed no signs of food preparation.

"I wanted you to leave Danny alone," she said, pulling a flank steak out of a pan of marinade and laying it flat on a platter. "He has something on his mind."

"I know he has," Jim answered, leaning against the wall. "As his best friend, it's my duty to find out what it is."

Maureen pulled two heads of lettuce out of the tiny refrigerator and began to make a salad.

"As a best friend it's your duty to mind your own business."

"Ah, come on, Mo." He leaned over and grabbed a leaf of lettuce from the colander and munched on it. "He hasn't said three sentences since he got here this afternoon." He reached for another leaf of romaine and his wife slapped his hand away. "I don't want to see him go through anything like he did after Michael was killed."

Maureen looked up from slicing tomatoes and shook her head. "It's nothing like that at all," she said, her short cape of dark curls bouncing merrily. "I know my brother pretty well—I think he's finally met someone."

Jim stared at her as if she had turned orange and sprouted wings.

"A woman?"

Maureen grinned, her dark blue eyes, sparkling against her tan. "Of course a woman—unless I know my brother less than I think."

"That secretive SOB," Jim said with a delighted laugh. "I'm gonna go up and ask Dan—"

"Ask Dan what?"

They both turned toward the stairwell and saw Dan's tall lean frame looming there.

Maureen shot Jim a look honed by six years of marriage.

"I wanted Jimmy to ask you if you want oil and vinegar or my extra special Russian dressing on your salad."

Dan laughed and squeezed into the tiny galley.

"Maureen Flanagan's Russian special," he said, grabbing a spear of romaine and eluding his sister's playful swat. "I can't think of anything I'd rather have."

Jim saw the funny, oddly soft look pass across his brother-in-law's face. He looked over at his wife, who flashed an "I- told-you-so" grin at him.

"Damn," he mumbled under his breath. "I think the guy's in love."

Seventy miles away Stefanie put her dessert fork down and glanced around the dining table at the faces of her family and wondered what on earth she was doing there. They were as familiar to her as her own face in the mirror each morning, and yet she felt totally isolated from the lot of them.

During the soup course her mother and her brother Harrison III discussed the latest ruling on taxes by the

Massachusetts Supreme Court. During the salad her father and her sister-in-law Madolyn argued the merits of the latest union demands laid before Colt Quarry, Inc. The main course accompanied a group discussion on defense spending led by her oldest brother, Walker, and dessert was sweetened with an argument *en famille* on the imminent failure of the Social Security system.

Issues, issues, and more issues. Even a discussion on Brendan and Katie's romance would have been preferable to the dreary bloodless passions her family preferred.

"So, Stefanie, how are things at Tele-Com going?"

She looked at Walker, whose light blue eyes were fastened on her with the myopic stare he reserved for the fine print in the *Wall Street Journal.* Obviously she was the topic for after-dinner coffee.

Suddenly the urge was overwhelming.

"I quit." She tried hard to keep the laughter out of her voice.

"You did what?" Elisabeth's well-modulated voice had risen at least an octave.

"Smartest move you've made, Stefanie," her father said, inhaling on his Cuban cigar. "You can have a vice presidency at Colt on Tuesday morning."

Madolyn, who was already a VP at Colt, gave her one of her model sister-in-law smiles. "Family should stick together," she said. "I've always wanted to work with you."

Harrison settled back in his chair and nodded at Stefanie as if she had finally awakened from a deep coma. "What are your plans now that you've left that Mickey Mouse company?"

She knew her eyes danced with suppressed laughter.

"Funny you should mention Mickey Mouse," she said, pushing her chair away from the table and rising. "I'm moving down to Orlando. I'm going to be one of those girls who strap you into the roller coaster at Disney World."

The room went totally still. They looked like clones, she thought. A tableful of blue-eyed blondes, all with their resolute Yankee jaws hanging open.

"If you'll excuse me, I'm going outside. There's a full moon tonight and I don't want to miss it."

She left the dining room and had barely gone five feet down the hall when she heard the explosion of sound from around the table.

"She must be kidding..."

"Maybe she's premenstrual—she *does* want to look at the moon..."

"I told her she's been acting strangely lately..."

She slipped outside into the yard.

"Congratulations." The male voice floated across the moonlit darkness. "That was quite an exit."

"Brendan?" She moved toward the marble bench at the end of the flagstone patio. "I thought you were out on the Cape with Katie."

Her brother, tall and mahogany-haired like herself, patted the side of the bench. She sat down next to him.

"Katie had a last-minute business dinner with a client at the Pru." The Prudential building with its good restaurant and great view of Boston was the latest meet-and-greet place for executives. "I thought I'd hang out awhile then pick her up and head out to Eastham."

"So what are you doing lurking about in the shadows?" She tossed her head in the direction of the house. "You should have been in there suffering along with me."

"I was about to come in and say hi when you started the Colt revolt. You were really rolling, Red."

"I don't know what came over me," she said with a laugh. "Maybe it *is* the full moon. I just couldn't listen to one more speech about the Dow Jones averages and union givebacks. I felt like a changeling in there." She rolled her eyes melodramatically. "Madolyn seems more like their daughter than I do."

Brendan put his arm around her and gave her a quick hug.

"Face it, Red. Mother found us under a copy of the *Harvard Law Review.*"

"That sounds like something Katie would say."

"She does say it. Repeatedly."

Stefanie laughed. "Do you think being a redhead has anything to do with it?"

He yanked a lock of her hair. "Probably has everything to do with it."

They were quiet for a while, listening to the faint rumbles of conversation from inside the big house. Much in the same way they found themselves outside the main house now, they had found themselves metaphorically sitting outside the family proper all their lives—a situation Brendan found amusing and Stefanie, until recently, found intolerable.

"How is Katie?" she asked. "It's been—what? Four months since I've seen her."

"Katie's fine." He grinned. "Terrific, actually."

"Is that a slightly prejudiced statement?"

"Definitely."

From nowhere an image of Dan as he leaned in her car window that afternoon appeared in the moonlit air before Stefanie.

"How does it feel?" It was more a statement than a question.

With the special telepathy common between twins, Brendan understood her shorthand.

"Do you remember that feeling you had on Christmas morning as a kid—you were giddy with excitement, absorbing pleasure through every pore?" He closed his eyes for a split second then looked at her. "That's how I feel every time Katie smiles at me—like it's Christmas morning."

Impulsively Stefanie threw her arms around her brother and hugged him tight.

"She's lucky to have you, Bren."

He returned the hug then shot a look at her wristwatch.

"Want to call and remind her of that? If I don't get moving, she'll never believe it."

Arm-in-arm they strolled through the damp backyard to the side of the house where the cars were parked.

"Should I tell the folks you were here?"

He shook his head. "I'm meeting them Friday for dinner in town. I mainly dropped by to touch base with you."

Her throat constricted with emotion. "What did I do to deserve a brother like you?"

"Nothing at all, probably," he said, opening the door to his Corvette. "In case you forgot, we came as a package deal."

They talked for a few minutes about the portfolio she'd gotten from Gabe Freeman, but Brendan told her just to leave it with their mother rather than go back inside the house to get it. He hugged her and she hung on a second longer than usual, hungry for the comfort only human touch can provide.

"Are you okay?" He moved back from her a fraction and looked at her, trying to read her expression in the darkness of the driveway. "You haven't been yourself lately, Red."

Stefanie chuckled and brushed the back of her hand across her forehead. "Now you're starting to sound like the rest of them," she teased.

"Is it work?" he persisted.

She hesitated.

"Is it love?"

"No such luck."

Their laughter broke the tension. She looked at her watch and gave him a gentle push.

"You'd better motor, little brother." She let the chance to tell her brother about Dan go by. "Katie's waiting."

He slid behind the wheel and started the engine.

"We're going to spend a weekend in Manhattan later this month," he said over the roar of the engine. "Why don't you meet Katie and me for dinner one night? We could even drive out to you, if you want."

"I'd love it. Just give me a couple days' notice, okay?"

Brendan nodded and, with a wave of his hand, backed out of the driveway and zoomed off toward his lady love.

Stefanie stood in the driveway for a few moments, drawing her sweater closer around her body. The full moon had risen higher in the night sky and the glow sparkling through the trees cast rippling shadows along the lawn. Inside the house the lights in the library flickered on and she moved deeper into the shadows, reluctant to give up her private thoughts to her very public family.

All evening Dan's face had hovered at the edge of her consciousness. She let it drift forward now until she could almost see him, illuminated by the moonlight, his eyes a darker blue than the September night sky.

She was too practical, too honest with herself not to recognize the way he had made her feel. When he leaned inside her car window to say good-bye, she had wanted him to kiss her and had been very disappointed when he didn't. Perhaps if she'd met him a year ago she just might have said yes to his invitation to spend the weekend on his friends' boat. For a moment she'd been tempted to discover what it would be like to be cradled in his strong arms for one glorious night. His presence was overwhelmingly dynamic, yet laced with a protectiveness that made her wonder if there were things she could learn from him that went far beyond the obvious.

A sense of well-being showered over her like the moonlight through the trees, and in that moment she knew Brendan was with Katie. She'd watched her brother change in the year he'd been seeing Katie from a slightly wild-with-the-women guy to a walking advertisement for the wonders of love. Beyond the undeniable excitement of falling in love, he had found the deep well of peace a human being needs to grow to his fullest. She envied him that.

Her career had been undeniably rewarding. Putting her mind and talents to use provided a sense of purpose she'd needed. However, she had always viewed the ability to love as one of life's major accomplishments, and so far she'd not had the opportunity to use her heart the way she'd used her mind.

The oak trees rustled and a jolt of fear rocketed through her.

"It's the wind, you fool," she said out loud. Nothing dangerous, nothing to cause that sudden, unthinking fear she fought back right now.

Dan said there was another way. She didn't have to be controlled by fear. She could learn to conquer it. But contacting him would be opening doors to something she was sure neither she nor Dan could control, something that would change their lives completely, and she didn't know if she had the courage to do that.

The full moon glittering above the Rhode Island Sound was so beautiful that Dan found it difficult to breathe over the swelling of his heart behind his breastbone.

Jim and Maureen had retired to their cabin a few hours ago. He had heard the low murmurs of conversation as they went below deck and the sweet sound of his sister's laugh before the cabin door closed behind them. Dan, however, had chosen to stay on deck, nursing a gin and tonic and a melancholy mood.

Had Jim and Maureen always seemed so much a unit, so obviously married? They'd been together seven years—six of them married—and Dan never remembered being so acutely aware of their relationship to one another.

Why hadn't he ever noticed the little looks, the verbal shorthand that punctuated their conversations? Did all couples somehow achieve this kind of intimacy after a certain length of time passed or were Jim and Mo somehow special?

He took a long swallow of his drink and stretched his legs out in front of him. He felt as if all of his nerve endings were exposed, alive to sensations he never knew existed.

In the darkness, the solitude, he was able to conjure up the firm set to Stefanie's jaw, the precise angle of her cheekbones. But he could also visualize her backed against her car, her fear as visible to him as if it were outlined by flame.

She wouldn't call him. To call him would be to lay bare her deepest fears, to admit to being vulnerable.

He hadn't been there when his brother needed him. All of his knowledge, all of his talents had been as nothing to keep his brother alive. With Stefanie, though, he would push against her boundaries, release her from the narrow prison of fear before it held her back any longer from realizing her full potential as a human.

He smiled into the darkness.

Her full potential as a woman.

5

Dan had been sitting in his Porsche in the parking lot of Conway News Service since eight fifteen. It was Tuesday morning, the day after Labor Day, and the first opportunity he had had to see Stefanie since their interlude on the ferry. He had tried to get there before eight to see her before she started work, but traffic delayed him. In fact, if he'd had his way, he would have been sitting in front of her apartment building the night before, waiting for her to return from her family weekend. Fortunately, however, good sense prevailed and he stayed away.

Besides, Jim and Maureen had been suspicious enough and the last thing he wanted was to reveal his feelings to anyone. Not yet. In fact, the whole weekend was a blur to him. His last clear memories were of Stefanie in her silver Toyota as she drove away to Boston, her red hair blowing from the open window.

He glanced at his watch. Nearly ten. He ran his long fingers through his dark curls, took a deep breath, then got out of his car, forgetting to lock the door behind him.

What if she wasn't there? he thought as he flashed his ID card at the security guard at the front door and was buzzed inside.

What if everything he thought she felt had been all wrong? he wondered as he scanned the information board for the international division, where he knew Gabe Freeman worked.

He was going to offer her a free course in self-defense—just thinking about that vulnerable look in her eyes made him know how badly she needed the knowledge. Even if she wasn't interested in him the way he hoped, he would at least be able to help erase the fears that ran through her, weakening her.

"Danny!"

A high female voice echoed down the long hall. Dan turned and faced a small blonde, her large blue eyes raking lazily over his body, lingering a little longer than necessary around the waistband of his tight jeans.

"Hi, Lori." He waved and continued walking.

"What's the hurry?" she persisted, her high heels clicking in pursuit. "Wait for me, Danny. I want to ask you something."

He stopped and jammed his thumbs into the low-slung pockets of his jeans, a buzz of annoyance vibrating through his body.

"I'm sorry I missed the last two classes," she said, looking up at him. "I hope you don't hold it against me."

"I hope you don't hold it against yourself," he answered, her efforts at flirtation wasted on him. "Staying safe isn't something you play games with. You either have the time or you don't."

Lori's face tightened. "Are you here to set up the next series of classes?"

He glanced at his watch, then at her. "I don't know if there's going to be a next series of classes here." He reached into the inside pocket of his leather jacket and handed her a business card. "This is my school's address and phone number. If you want to schedule something, my secretary will be glad to set you up in a self-defense course."

She fingered the card, flicking it against her chin.

"Do you teach all of the classes? You are the most marvelous—"

"I have six highly qualified teachers. Any one of us would suit your purposes."

With a nod he hurried off toward the international division on the second floor.

Women like Lori never called, never showed up for the real thing. They gave lip service to safety, but they viewed a self-defense course as nothing more than a great way to meet single men. He'd rather let his instructors handle that. In a world where people were attacked for radios and eyeglasses, it was more important for him to give his time to people who really cared.

In every seminar he held, there was always one person who approached him after class and quietly, apologetically, told him about the time he or she had been a victim. Invariably he thought of his brother Michael and his stomach would twist at the injustice of it all.

Usually Dan waited to be approached, but with Stefanie he found that impossible. He knew he was right about her—there was no mistaking the essence of fear. It clung to a person like a scent you could never eradicate. She needed to be free of it and he needed to be the person to show her how.

He took the stairs two at a time and hurried down the corridor. The office at Conway was casual; secretaries hurried along in cords or faded jeans, others in pin-striped dress-for-success uniforms. Engineers in baggy khakis mingled with accountants in sober blue suits. Each one was identified by his uniform as surely as if a sign hung around his or her neck. In tight faded jeans, black T-shirt, and leather jacket, Dan could have been mistaken for one of the installers or technicians were it not for the almost palpable air of self-assurance, of power, that radiated from him. He had the kind of magnetism that caused women to stop speaking when he walked by, that caused men to glance at him a second time, envying him his sense of self, something no three-piece suit or master's degree could bestow.

The doors to some of the offices were closed and none of them bore any identifying marks besides a metal number attached to the frame. Stefanie hadn't been listed by name on the directory and he didn't know Gabe's last name. This was the international development division—at least that he was sure of.

"Hey! Excuse me." He stopped an older man in shirt-sleeves who passed him in the hall. "Do you know where Stefanie Colt's office is?"

The man scratched his head with a pencil he had nestled behind his ear. "Colt? Colt? Oh, yeah—that's the rep from Tele-Com." He pointed toward a staircase at the end of the corridor. "Down one flight, last office on your left."

Dan thanked him and the man moved away, muttering to himself about cost overruns and inflated estimates. Dan went back down the stairs. Rep from Tele-Com? What in hell was Tele-Com? Here he'd had her figured for a secretary or something and it seemed she was some kind of representative from another firm. What if she'd only been there for the day? The thought that she might have disappeared from his life sent a thrill of fear through his body that he quickly dismissed. He wouldn't let that happen—he wasn't the kind of man who allowed things like that to happen to him.

This floor was much like the one above it, with unmarked doors, some open, some not. The same bustle of workers scurrying around. He stopped just before the closed door to her office and smoothed his black T-shirt into the waistband of his jeans, readjusted the sleeves on his leather jacket, drew his fingers through his hair in a futile attempt to control it. He could no more control the dark curls than he could control the rush of anticipation that coursed through his body.

He lifted his hand and knocked on the glass inset of the door.

Stefanie was sitting at her desk, nursing her third cup of coffee and a growing case of caffeine nerves.

All of the problems she had ironed out so neatly on Friday evening had developed new wrinkles over the weekend and she was praying she wouldn't have to schedule a trip to L.A. to see what was happening with Tele-Com's relay system out there. She'd been on the phone since seven o'clock with her support team at the home office and they were trying to convince her that she needed either to go out to L.A. or come to them in Omaha for new hands-on experience on the R25A relay system they were putting into operation for Conway.

She sipped the coffee, grimaced, then tore open another packet of Sweet 'N Low, dumping the powder into her Styrofoam cup and stirring it. She took another sip, then pushed the whole mess to the other side of her desk. At that point she didn't know what was worse, her coffee or her job.

Face it, she thought, getting up and standing by her window, tracing her finger along the dusty sill, *you've run out of excuses. Either you get moving, or you get out.*

Her job deserved more than halfway measures and half of herself was all she had to offer at this point. If she could just postpone all trips until her contract came due, maybe she simply wouldn't renegotiate. There were plenty of other companies around who'd welcome someone with her credentials onto their team. What did she need with this traveling, these headaches, anyway? Was there anything so terrible about taking the easy way out just once in her life?

But there was still the trip to Hawaii in November, two months away; and there was no one else qualified to go. She was deep in thought, trying to come up with a solution, and she jumped at the sound of a sharp series of three knocks at her door.

"Yes?" Her voice was crisp, slightly unwelcoming.

The door swung open. Her head was bent over a stack of papers on her credenza. "Can I help you?" she asked, not looking up.

"No, but I think I can help you."

Her heart leaped into her throat at the sound of his rough, wrong-side-of-Boston voice.

He loomed in the doorway to her office, all six-feet-three of him, dark and dangerous in a leather jacket that would make her family reach for the phone to call the police. She sank into her chair, mesmerized by the way his body tapered from broad shoulders down to an impossibly tiny waist. A vision of him in his *gi*, the springy curls of chest hair visible through the deep V of the top, danced in front of her, and she smiled.

"Does that mean I can sit down?"

She shook her head to clear away the cobwebs.

"I can't?"

"No. No, of course you can. I was just daydreaming."

"Something pleasant, I hope?" He sat down and leaned back in the chair, his legs stretching under her desk until the tips of his boots touched the heel of her shoe.

"Oh, yes," she answered, brushing her hair off her face and wishing she could check her makeup. "Something very pleasant. Can I get you some coffee?"

"Is it better than the coffee they had on the ferry?"

She got up and adjusted the skirt of her dark gold dress.

"It's warmer," she said, crossing over to the credenza. "That's the best I can say about it."

He switched around in his seat and she could feel his eyes on her as she poured him a cup of coffee.

"Cream and sugar?" she asked over one shoulder.

"Black."

She turned around to walk back to her desk but stopped in her tracks. His eyes were fastened on her legs.

"Do I have a run in my stockings?" She looked down, searching. "It's rude to stare like that, Dan."

His smile was wide, his teeth white and gleaming against his dark mustache and beard.

"Don't blame me. You've got great legs, Stefanie."

She stood still for a moment, clutching the Styrofoam cup of hot black coffee. Then, without warning, laughter bubbled up as if from some forgotten spring. Her shoulders shook with it and she had to lean against the side of her desk for support. There was no subterfuge with this man—he said what he thought and meant what he said. He was a delight.

Dan laughed along with her at first, even though he was unsure exactly what the joke was. Stefanie's body was shuddering with mirth and some of the coffee sloshed over the side of the container and splashed onto the fabric of her dress. He jumped up and put the container on her desk, then grabbed a handful of Kleenex from the holder on the credenza.

"Let me," she said, her laughter barely daunted by the spill. She reached for the Kleenex he was about to dip in a pitcher of iced water. "Water ruins silk."

"And I suppose coffee's good for it?"

He slipped his hand beneath the hem of her dress and held the flared skirt slightly away from her body. The back of his hand brushed against her stockinged thigh and her laughter disappeared in a quick intake of breath. He was down before her on one knee, his head so close to her that she could feel his breath warm on her leg. His hand moved slightly upward against her thigh and she wondered what he would think if he discovered she was wearing stockings, rather than the asexual armor of panty hose. She'd ruined her last pair of panty hose that morning and had reached for the garter belt and stockings she'd bought on a whim a year ago in Paris.

"The stain seems lighter," he said, reaching for another tissue and dipping it into the cold water. "The water helped. The dress might survive."

She looked down into his dark blue eyes as his shoulder brushed against her hip and felt, at that moment, that she would do anything he asked just so she could feel him close to her.

"I hope I survive," she murmured, as he resumed dabbing at the stain in a way that was simultaneously awkwardly masculine and tremendously tender.

"What was that?"

She cleared her throat. "I said, it's been a rough day so far. I hope I survive it."

He looked up again, his thick dark brows arching in question. "It's only ten thirty, Stefanie. How rough a day can it have been?"

She grabbed the edge of her desk for support.

"You'd be surprised," she answered, trying desperately to smother the urge to touch his shining hair.

He had just finished doing what he could for the coffee stain and was about to take his hand away and let her skirt drop down to its just-below-the-knee length, when the office door swung open and Gabe Freeman, flushed and carrying a sheaf of papers, came into the room.

"Hey, Colt, I—" He stopped in midsentence. His eyes bulged behind the lenses of his wire-rimmed glasses.

Later on Stefanie had to admit it looked pretty incriminating—there she was, pressed back against the desk, hands clutching the edges in a white-knuckled grasp, her face showing who-knew-what wild emotion. And Dan—Dan was kneeling in front of her, his large hand snaking its way up her skirt.

Well, it was no wonder Gabe had pounced on him like a tiger.

"I didn't know you desk jockeys had it in you," Dan said after he'd helped Gabe up from the floor and handed him the wire-rimmed glasses that had fallen off during their tussle. He rubbed his shoulder, which had struck the edge of the desk when Gabe landed on him. "Do you work out?"

Gabe shook his head, grimacing at the pain shooting through muscles unaccustomed to action. "Don't believe in it." He glanced over at Stefanie, who sat perched on her desk, patting at the coffee stain on her skirt. "Going back and forth to the water cooler is aerobic enough for me."

Stefanie, feeling awkward over the misunderstanding, looked at Dan. "Don't let Gabe's modesty fool you. Under that three-piece suit lies the heart of Supersalesman."

Gabe's brown eyes went from Stefanie to Dan then back to Stefanie, assessing. Now he could see that he'd been wrong: The look in her eyes wasn't fear at all. It had been bemusement, wonder, perhaps a touch of desire. The story about the coffee stain had been true, but there had been more—a hell of a lot more—going on in that room besides the mopping up of coffee.

"Uh, listen, I've got a meeting with the guys in corporate engineering. I'll just leave these papers for your signature, Stef, and shove off."

"The meeting with corporate!" Stefanie jumped off the desk. "I'm supposed to make a presentation to them at noon." She hurried to the lateral file in the corner of the room, yanked out a sheaf of manila folders filled with reports, then went back to her desk. "Push them back till one, would you, Gabe? Since I didn't make the trip to Dayton, I have to bone up on the figures for the new cable."

Gabe nodded. He readjusted his glasses with his middle finger. That O'Connor guy was making no move to leave. Stefanie looked up and met Gabe's eyes. She smiled. *It's okay,* her look said. *Really.*

Sighing, he turned to Dan. "I still don't know how you flipped me like that," he said. "Damnedest thing I ever saw."

Dan grinned. "I wasn't trying to hurt you," he said. "I just wanted to get you the hell off me so I could figure out what was going on." He thought for a second. "Listen, if you really want to know how I did it, I'm doing a six-week course here in late October. Why don't you come?"

"I work late most nights." Gabe's voice was regretful. "I only have weekends."

"I have a school in Northport." He mentioned the street and Gabe nodded. "We have Saturday classes. Why don't you come down and try them—on the house?"

All suspicions about Dan vanished. Gabe's broad face lit up with a smile. He reached out and shook Dan's hand heartily.

"That's real nice of you. I'll do just that. Thanks."

Stefanie looked up from the pile of papers on her desk. "If you two don't mind, I have some work to do."

Gabe had a healthy respect for Stefanie's temper and, after getting a business card from Dan with the class hours penciled in, he hurried out of the office. Dan, however, stayed behind, settling down in one of the leather chairs adjacent to her desk, his long legs stretched out in front of him. He picked up an issue of *Time* from the magazine rack and noisily flipped through it.

At the sound of his cough, Stefanie glanced up.

"Dan!" She sounded startled. "I thought you left with Gabe."

He shook his head. "I wasn't finished talking to you. If you remember, we got sidetracked."

She grew warm, her thoughts floating to the way his hand had felt against her leg.

"Why did you laugh before?" He picked up where they had left off.

"I'd rather not say."

"Now you have to tell me. You've got me thinking you're making fun of me."

She leaned forward and touched his arm. "Oh, no, Dan, I wasn't. Really." She hesitated. "I've simply never met a man as, shall we say, direct as you are."

"Your legs?"

"My legs."

"I can't believe no one's ever told you you have great legs before."

"Let's say no one was ever that blunt before."

"Why not? Are your Harvard men too polite to tell a woman they like what they see?"

"No. They're just more circumspect." He didn't say anything. "They're more cautious," she elaborated.

"I know what the word means, Stefanie." His voice was low, measured.

She turned deep red, suddenly aware of the gaps in privilege between them.

"I'm sorry. When you didn't say anything, I assumed—"

"Assumed that since I don't have a degree, I need an interpreter?"

"I assumed no such thing. Don't foist your own insecurities onto me, Dan. Lack of a degree doesn't mean a thing to me."

He got up and leaned over the desk.

"You have one, don't you?"

Stefanie nodded.

"In what?"

"Computer engineering."

"Just a bachelor's?"

She squirmed. "No. I have a master's from MIT."

His face darkened, the blue eyes turning almost black. "Ask me where I went to school, why don't you?"

She swallowed.

"This is ridiculous, Dan." She went to stand up but he loomed over her, so large and terrifying and obviously not about to move that she sat back down again. "What difference does it make? I don't care where you went to school."

"I didn't go to school," he said, watching her face.

"Not everyone needs a college degree."

He grinned. "I'm not talking about college, Stefanie."

"High school?"

He nodded.

"You dropped out?"

He nodded again.

"When?"

"In the middle of junior year."

"Why?"

He shrugged. "It was a long time ago. Let's say I was a different person then."

She couldn't imagine what could have forced him to drop out of high school. She'd never known anyone who didn't have a high school diploma—something she considered as basic to a person's development as taking his first steps or learning the alphabet.

"Do you regret it?" she asked, certain that he must.

"Do you regret not being married?"

"What does that have to do with anything?"

"You don't miss what you've never had, right?"

Her words slipped out uncensored. "I do."

His senses were instantly alerted.

"Tell me."

Those dark eyes were hypnotic. They were riveted to her and she had no choice but to speak. She wanted to speak.

"I'd like to be married. I know I'd love to have a family. It's something I've always wanted."

The urge to touch her shot through his body and he had to fight it down. He pointed around the office, at the accoutrements of her success.

"This isn't enough for you?" He was baiting her.

"Should it be?"

"Why not! Great job, probably a great salary. Freedom—most women would think you're pretty lucky."

She pushed her hair back from her face. "I like to think I'm not 'most women.'"

You're not, he thought. *You're not like any woman I've ever known before.*

"You don't like your job?" he asked.

"I used to like it very much," she said. "But a career can't be your whole life, can it?"

"You tell me."

She'd never verbalized these thoughts before and her voice was soft, slower than her normal rapid-fire delivery.

"No," she said finally. "Not for me. Tele-Com can't go home with me at night. I can't love a company the way I could love a husband. A family." She brushed her words aside as if they were pesky flies buzzing around her head. "But I'm sure you didn't come here to talk about my thoughts on home and hearth. What did you want to see me about, Dan?"

He recognized a closed door when he saw one. There would be time enough for it to open again.

"I'd like you to come to class tonight, Stefanie."

"Learn karate? I don't really think I—"

"Don't think. Just listen: You told me you're afraid. Hell, I saw it written on your face last week. Give me two hours tonight." He stood up and walked around the side of her desk. He bent down in front of her until his limitless eyes were on a level with hers. "You don't have to live with fears, Stefanie. They don't have to win."

"Maybe another time."

"No."

He reached for her hands and held them in his. He could feel the trembling in her slender fingers. "Just two hours, Stefanie. Give me that."

She was strong-willed but he was stronger. His force obliterated all of her excuses and left her, vulnerable and exposed, just to nod her head in agreement.

"Want me to pick you up?"

She pulled her hands away from his.

"Afraid I won't show up?"

"The thought had occurred to me."

She looked him full in the face, willing her green eyes to hide her fear.

"I'll be there, Dan. You have my word."

He nodded, then stood up, still very close to her. His thighs and hips were on a level with her eyes and she found her gaze magnetized by his lean body. His legs were long and covered by faded jeans so tight she wondered how he could move with such agility, such grace. His waist was narrow and taut and the leather jacket emphasized the classic V of his proportions. She wanted to touch him, to run her hands along his body, to see if she would incinerate at the feel of him beneath her fingertips. . . .

She cleared her throat.

"What time is the class?"

He grinned. "Eight o'clock."

She smiled back at him. "What do I wear?"

"Loose pants and a T-shirt or sweat shirt. Comfortable clothes. Or—" the grin was broader now "—you could always wear a *gi*."

She shot him her best upper-class look. "You must be joking."

He bent down once again and cupped her chin in his hand. His flesh was hot against hers and she pressed closer to it for an instant.

"You may be surprised tonight, Stefanie. You might learn a few things about yourself that MIT couldn't teach you."

Before she could answer he was gone, and all that remained was the warmth of his hand against her face and an electric excitement that charged the air of her small office.

6

All afternoon Stefanie toyed with the idea of not showing up. The thought of actually taking a karate class sent her stomach into acrobatics the flying Wallenda family would have coveted. While Dan was in her office, mesmerizing her with his hypnotic gaze, she would have promised him anything. However, once he left and she returned to the level of ordinary life, her fears and inhibitions took hold again and she questioned the wisdom of showing up that evening.

There's no point in going, she thought as she tore through her dresser and closet, searching for clothes that would be comfortable yet attractive.

Dan's a better salesman than anyone working for Tele-Com, Stefanie thought as she backed her car out of the driveway and headed east on Route 25A.

All the reasons why she should stay away and all the reasons why she had to go battled inside her. She even drove around the block twice before making a left turn into the parking lot behind his school. She didn't exactly believe in karma the way Brendan's Katie did, but maybe there was something to the notion of fate.

Some thing, some force, had made it impossible for her to stay home tonight, to barricade herself behind her locks and bolts and alarm systems. She turned off the engine and sat behind the wheel, taking deep rhythmic breaths to control her nerves.

He said that they, the dangers of the world, don't have to win.

She was there to make him prove it.

It took only moments for her to realize she should have accepted Dan's offer of a *gi*. She sat on the floor of the *dojo,* or training room, feeling as if she'd shown up in her underwear at a fancy dress ball. All of the other women were clad in the comfortable, unobtrusive white cotton outfits. A few men, also in *gis,* stood at the far end of the room. One of them had a brown belt sashed around his waist, the other two were belted in blue. Most of the students, though, wore the white sash of the rank beginner. She looked ridiculous in the dark brown running outfit that had seemed so right in her bedroom mirror.

"Excuse me." A woman's voice broke into her thoughts.

Stefanie turned toward a brunette in her midthirties who was doing stretching exercises next to her.

"Yes?"

The woman arched her back and touched her head with her right foot. Stefanie tried not to stare in frank amazement.

"First class?" the woman asked, straightening up.

Stefanie laughed and gestured toward her running outfit. "It shows, doesn't it?"

The woman gave a quick smile, then pointed at Stefanie's feet. "The sneakers," she said with a glance toward the door leading from the office to the *dojo*. You'd better get them off before *Sensei* gets in here."

"*Sensei?*" Stefanie frowned. "Oh—that's right. Dan."

A questioning look flickered over the other woman's face at Stefanie's familiar use of Dan's name.

"I'd get them off as quick as I could and stash 'em in the closet over there, if I were you. *Sensei*'s a stickler on proper form."

The Dan she'd met hardly seemed one to play by the rules, Stefanie thought, as she yanked off her worn Nikes and tossed them in the closet. The Dan she'd met seemed more inclined to break them.

She'd expected a noisier atmosphere, something more in keeping with a gym, and the woman's stressing proper form emphasized how unexpectedly formal Dan's school was. She looked around the room. There were about fifteen women in the class, varying in age from high school to late middle-age. They chatted quietly in small groups. Some of them performed stretching routines as the woman next to her had.

Not even the decor was what she had expected. It was simple, almost stark, with that tranquil undercurrent she'd always associated with the Orient. The walls of the high-ceilinged room were paneled in a very light oak that was balanced by the thickly padded dark brown carpeting on the floor. In one corner, a built-in air conditioner hummed quietly, while an enormous gray vinyl punching bag swung from a hook in the ceiling in the opposite corner. A flag of Japan hung next to the Stars and Stripes on the long wall opposite her, surrounding what looked like two wooden nightsticks attached by a leather thong.

She found herself obsessed with the visual details of the room. Anything to keep her mind off exactly what she was doing there. The world outside paid no attention to ritual and form. The posturing of a collection of judo groupies could hardly matter out there. Guns and knives still existed and she wondered what Dan would really be able to do for her.

The door to the *dojo* squeaked and she turned as Dan, wearing the black *gi* she had first seen him in at Conway, entered the room, bowing in the doorway in the direction of the flags. Everyone stood and she got to her feet, lining up against the long wall next to the woman who had cautioned her about her sneakers. Her eyes were fastened securely on Dan, wishing for some sign of recognition, an acknowledgment that he was aware of her presence in the room. He seemed distant, however, distracted, as if he'd entered deeper into himself in preparation for the class.

He took his place in the center of the room, legs apart, head bowed. The recessed fluorescent lights overhead picked up the random silver strands in his dark curls and for a second her breath caught in her throat. Waves of energy seemed to radiate around him, as if he were drawing all the electricity in the room into his body, so he could intensify it then let it flow back into the room, into the students.

A blond man of medium height and build, a brown belt tied loosely around the waistline of his white *gi,* bowed to Dan, then took his place at Dan's right side. He looked at the class. Her heart began to thud in anticipation and dread.

"Hands at side." He turned to Dan. *"Sensei, rei."*

Dan nodded. His hands, clenched in loose fists, were at waist level.

The brown belt looked back out at the class.

"Rei."

The students mimicked Dan's movements. They brought their clenched hands to waist level, then bowed in a gesture of respect that Stefanie, slightly annoyed at the feeling of subservience the bow caused, imitated somewhat clumsily. It didn't matter that Dan bowed to them simultaneously. The sensation of servility went against her grain.

He motioned for them to be seated and she settled herself on the heavily cushioned floor, resting her back against the wall and tucking her feet beneath her. He shot her a quick glance and she searched for some signal, some indication that he was glad she was there—some indication that he even saw her.

He looked back at the rest of the class.

She wrapped her arms around her chest.

I'll stick it out tonight, she thought, wishing he could read her mind. *I don't have to do this ever again.*

He hooked his thumbs in the black belt that held the top part of his *gi* together. It gaped open, exposing part of his tanned chest. This time, instead of intriguing her, the sight of his muscular body made her furious.

"In the past two weeks we've covered the importance of kicking, the elements of blocking, and palm strikes."

His eyes moved slowly around the room, making contact briefly with each student.

She watched him as his eyes rested on a pretty young blonde; a sophisticated brunette; a woman with short, sandy hair. When his eyes met hers and betrayed none of the intimacy he'd shown in her office a few hours earlier, her irritation increased.

He continued. "The one thing we haven't talked about yet is how you can avoid ever having to use anything I've taught you." There was a rush of nervous laughter from some of the women. Dan waited a moment before going on. His eyes met Stefanie's for a second and she sat up straighter, leaning forward. "The palm strike is an important—and highly effective—weapon in self-defense, but the best weapon you own is your own mind."

He began to walk up and down the length of the room, his bare feet sinking in the carpeting then reappearing with each step. "Let's face it: The older you get, the weaker you become, and the weaker you become, the more you have to rely on your mind. You're lucky—I'm going to teach you how to capitalize on this while you're still young and strong. I'm not interested in giving you green belts or brown belts. I don't give a damn if you have a belt at all. What I do give a damn about is that you leave here with a clear understanding of your own responsibility in defending yourself."

Dan stopped and looked down, those dark eyes of his focused somewhere beyond any woman in the room. He seemed to be drawing strength from deep inside himself. She could feel his magnetism, strong and pulsating, charging the air in the room. She could almost swear the fine hairs on her forearms tingled with it. He exuded a mesmerizing allure that was potentially more dangerous to her than anything on the street.

"Reality isn't some macho competition nor is it a win-or-lose situation. You're not going to be judged on perfect form, on your grace of agility. You'll learn techniques that will enable you to create exactly what you need when you need it. If you stay safe, we've done our job." He opened his hands, palms facing outward. "I hope you never have to throw a punch. I hope you never need to. Controlling a person's mind is the first step to controlling his body, and when you control his body, you control the situation. His dynamite grin exploded without warning and Stefanie felt the aftershock ricochet through her body. "Okay. Now get up and pair off and start practicing punches."

The class laughed at the irony of his words, then broke into groups to work on their palm strikes. In the three weeks the course had been in progress, partnerships had obviously been formed and Stefanie found herself standing alone near the closet door. She was tempted to pluck her Nikes out and sprint for the door, but instead she wrapped her arms around her chest against the cold blast of air from the air conditioner and stood there, waiting.

Dan moved from cluster to cluster, offering advice, refining techniques. She watched his face, intent on his work, and saw no sign of the lighthearted man who'd been in her office that morning. He must have felt her eyes on him because he looked up, caught her glance, then walked over to where she stood.

"You came."

"Yes, Dan, I did."

"I'm glad," he continued, "but I have to correct you on something."

She grinned and pointed toward her running outfit.

"Improper attire?"

He shook his head, smiling slightly.

"Not that. This class is a highly structured environment, and, as a gesture of respect, the teacher is referred to only as *Sensei* while in this room."

She hadn't felt that embarrassed since she was seven years old and had been caught sticking her tongue out at her teacher. She nodded and silently vowed she'd call him nothing quicker than she'd ever call him *Sensei*.

"They're doing their palm strikes," he said, leading her by the arm into an open space at the far side of the room, "but you're not ready for that yet. First, I have to teach you how to block the quadrants."

"Quadrants?" She smiled at him. "Sounds like something on the space shuttle."

He was all business. Apparently he left his sense of humor at home with his jeans and T-shirt.

"Watch me." He took the wide-legged stance she was becoming accustomed to, bent his knees, then lowered his head. "Okay. Now I block my left side—" his right arm bisected his body on a diagonal, shielding his left torso and head "—and now the right." He reversed his movements. "Now the low blocks." He hunkered down and demonstrated blocking the pelvic area and each leg. "Now you."

She planted her feet a shoulder's width apart and raised her right arm across the center of her body.

"Bend low," he said, putting his hands on her waist. "Lower your center of gravity, make it harder to get knocked off-balance."

She nodded, afraid her voice would betray the strange sensations his hands on her body were causing.

"Once more. Block the left side."

She again brought her right arm across her body, elbow jutting out at an awkward angle.

He stepped behind her, not pushing his body close but making her aware of his presence nonetheless. He lifted her right arm by the wrist and drew an index finger along the outside of her forearm.

"You feel this bone?"

"Yes." Oh, yes, she felt that bone. Right then, that long bone in her forearm was the center of every degree of heat in her body.

"Keep that bone turned outward. Let it absorb the blow. You'll be surprised how much stress it can take."

"Won't it break?"

"Not if the angle's right."

"I find that hard to believe," she said as he released her.

"Trust me."

He stepped in front of her to watch what she was doing as she practiced blocking, alternating from right side to left.

"Lower your head," he said. "Protect your face."

She continued putting up the blocks, feeling awkward and off-balance as she tried to cover the lower portion of her body.

"Stop." He stepped back a few feet and stood directly in front of her. "I want you to block what you see."

Her eyes widened. "I don't see anything," she said, praying to retain the status quo.

"I'm going to throw some punches at you."

Her stomach lurched.

"I don't think I can."

"You're not supposed to think. I give you the direction; just let your body respond to it."

He began to throw punches at her, not close enough to make contact, but close enough for her to feel the air-rush of violence around her. He threw a series of two quick rights and she missed both of them. She threw her arms up in the air.

"No more," she said. "I can't do this. I'm just not coordinated enough."

He grabbed her arm. Her fingers dug into the soft flesh of her upper arm.

"You don't have a choice."

Anger, clean as a sharp wind, whipped through her as she yanked her arm away from him. There would be bruises but she didn't care.

"Like hell I don't."

His face was closed to her, the blue eyes darker than ever.

"Okay, then—it's up to you, Stefanie. Do you want to learn, or do you want to pretend to learn? You can't have it both ways."

Some of the women on the other side of the room were watching them, their faces clearly expressing curiosity. Stefanie's anger was cooled by embarrassment.

"Fine, *Sensei*," she said, drawing out the strange word sarcastically. "Now what?"

"I'm punching for real this time. Now: Block!"

The punches were rhythmic, predictable, easy to block. She settled in and found herself anticipating his moves by watching the way his shoulder tightened before he threw a punch. The solid muscle of his left shoulder moved beneath the fabric of the *gi* and she quickly raised her left arm to block his punch, only to find a right coming at her. She froze as she realized she'd guessed wrong and his fist was coming straight at her.

Fortunately he was all too familiar with the newcomer's freeze and had pulled back before making contact.

"You were guessing, weren't you?" he asked, the beginning of a grin tilting his full mouth.

"No, I wasn't guessing," she answered. Her annoyance hid the vulnerability she was feeling. "I could tell exactly what you were going to throw by watching your shoulder muscles."

His grin broke across his face full force.

"Apparently your system has a few flaws."

She shrugged. "Well, you distracted me when you moved your left hand before you threw the punch."

He folded his arms across his chest. His dark eyes glittered.

"And I suppose you think that was unfair?"

She glared up at him.

"You suppose right, Dan—excuse me, *Sensei.*"

She knew her sarcastic tone wasn't lost on him by the way his eyes narrowed as he watched her.

"You have all the answers, haven't you, Stefanie?" He untied the black belt and his *gi* fell open, exposing his broad chest and its cover of curly black hair. He handed her the sash. "Here. Take it. If your system's so good, why don't you get up there and teach the class?"

His voice had gotten louder in his anger and a few of the other students were openly watching them.

"What are you waiting for, Stefanie? Not so sure of yourself now?"

She turned away from the students so they couldn't see the embarrassed flush that spread across her neck and face.

"Will you lower your voice, please? You're creating a scene." She pushed the black belt into his hands.

He took it, running his fingers across the length of heavy cotton material before retying it around his waist.

"This isn't a game," he said. She took note that he had lowered his voice as she'd asked.

"I never thought it was."

He touched her hand for a split second and in his dark blue eyes she saw that she was important to him.

For some strange reason, she mattered. Delight rushed through her body.

"Put your ego aside just for tonight and listen to me." His eyes never left hers. "We're not in competition, you know."

He softened his words with a smile. Unerringly he had zeroed in on the core of the problem. She had entered the class hell-bent on proving she didn't need the class at all, certain there was nothing of value he could show her. Admitting her own vulnerability, her need for knowledge, cut too close to the bone.

"I'll try," she said at last. "But I can't make any promises."

"I'm not asking for any." He paused. "Not now."

He moved a few steps back from her.

"Get into your defensive posture. Bend those knees. . . ." His face seemed to close in upon itself and she saw Dan absorbed into the persona of *sensei.* "Don't try to guess, don't watch my arms. Center yourself on the middle of my body and block only what you see, not what you think you will see."

Stefanie focused her eyes on the center of his chest, right above the spot where the top of his *gi* stopped. His punches came slowly at first and she found it difficult to keep from glancing at his arms and shoulders and face for a clue which punch would come next. Suddenly they came faster, out of sync. Rhythm disappeared, and she found her field of vision narrowing as her conscious mind turned control over to her body.

And her body didn't fail her. Her blocks came sure and strong. With each "thwack" against her forearm, a tingle of exhilaration coursed through her, hinting at all she had yet to learn.

"Okay, fine." He stopped throwing punches and nodded at her. "Not bad."

She wiped away a layer of sweat that had beaded her forehead beneath her bangs.

"Not bad? I was sensational!" The adrenaline rush of excitement heightened the color of her skin and made the gold flecks in her green eyes glitter like precious metal.

Beside her Dan cleared his throat, his own eyes skimming gently over her face like a pebble on the surface of a lake.

He excused himself for a moment and went over to his instructors. She watched his hands, so terrifyingly large yet so graceful, emphasizing his words as he gave instructions to them for the class. She noticed the looks some of the younger women cast in her direction, looks filled with curiosity and a touch of envy. It was apparent by their reactions that *Sensei* was not in the habit of giving private lessons.

She was still smiling when Dan, serious and intense, strode back over to her, his dark curls tumbling over his forehead in a way that made her yearn to brush them back.

"You don't have to give me special treatment, D— *Sensei*. I don't mind being a little behind the others."

"I mind."

Her head jerked up and she looked at him.

"I beg your pardon?"

"It's not fair to the others if we have to alter the class to let you catch up."

Her face burned with embarrassment. So much for special treatment, for being important. She willed herself to cool off, not to let him see how close she had come to letting him see inside her heart.

She lifted her chin, jaw tightening.

"Fine," she answered. "Then perhaps we should get on with it." She thanked her parents and the long line of cool Yankees who came before them for her ability to recover her poise.

Dan went over to the closet where she'd stashed her running shoes earlier and pulled out a square of wood cushioned and covered by dark blue vinyl. He curled his hand around one edge and supported the rest of the board against the inside of his forearm.

"See how I'm holding this?"

She nodded. He handed it to her.

"I'm going to throw palm strikes at it. I want you to see how much power you have a your command by using the heel of your palm as a weapon."

The blows were hard, sharp, perfectly centered on the padded board. The board absorbed much of the shock, but she still had to bend her knees and brace herself for impact of each blow.

"You make it seem so easy," she said as they traded places.

"It *is* easy. Who said it had to be difficult to be effective?"

She took a deep breath, her hands palm up at her waist, her eyes on Dan.

"Don't watch me," he said. "Focus on a point past the board and go for it."

She threw a right, her blow landing with a dull thud.

"Oh, God," she said with a moan. "I can't do it. I don't seem to have the strength."

The crack of a punch landing on a board across the *dojo* drew her attention. A small blond woman of about thirty was smiling triumphantly at her partner who held the board.

Stefanie looked back at Dan and gave a good-natured shrug.

"It's not a matter of strength, hmm?"

"You got it." He didn't smile but the light in his eyes gave his true sentiments away.

For fifteen minutes he coached her on blending softness with hardness, on not telegraphing her intentions to an aggressor, on starting her movements slowly, unthreateningly, then concentrating all of her force into the punch just before contact to maximize both its shock value and physical impact.

Stefanie began to enjoy herself. The knowledge that there was an alternative to surrender was just beginning to seem real to her, and its possibilities made her feel strong, less frightened than she had in months. As they worked together on making her body respond instantly to a threat, she found herself filled with a grudging admiration for Dan and his abilities. There was nothing of the showman about him, no grandiose leaps through the air, no macho displays of chest-beating. What there was was unshakable confidence, a high-voltage strength that sizzled its way into her limbs and made her feel invincible.

"Okay," he said finally, "you've got it."

She threw a quick right-left combination into the air between them.

"I'll take that black belt now if it's still available," she teased, restraining herself from singing out with pleasure at her sudden, potent awareness of her body as an instrument she could teach to work with her mind.

He glanced down at her and shook his head.

"Let's work on getting you into a *gi* first, okay?"

She grinned at him, not caring that everyone else in the *dojo* was listening to their conversation with an intensity usually reserved for the popular TV series "Dynasty."

He motioned for her to join the rest of the class once more and he headed for the center of the room. He did a quick review of defensive postures and the importance of using one's hands to maintain one's body space. Stefanie tried to concentrate on his words but found herself drawn instead to the emotion behind the words, to the man behind the teacher.

He ran through a series of kung fu postures to emphasize the difference between self-defense courses and the cultural study of the martial arts and she was amazed at the beauty and grace inherent in the male body as he curved his arm and hand into the beak of a bird, the wing of a dove.

The instructor with the dark blond hair glanced at the clock that hung over the swinging doors.

"Thirty minutes more, *Sensei*."

Dan glanced up at the clock himself, as if he couldn't believe time had so quickly elapsed.

"I wanted to cover getting out of chokes," he said to the brown belt.

He turned back to the class. "Sit down and relax. Mike and I are going to show you a few holds and escapes. Hold your questions until after, okay?"

The two men smoothly went through a synchronized routine of grabs and releases that were beautifully executed but, to Stefanie, proved essentially nothing.

"Any questions?"

"It was an impressive show," she said, "but how realistic was it?"

Dan looked at her, his eyes registering surprise at her comment.

"What do you mean?"

"Well, what you showed us was great, but you're both men. You're matching strength against strength."

The other students looked from Stefanie to Dan and back again, heads swiveling like spectators at Wimbledon.

"I thought I explained to you that mind is more important that muscle in my system."

She leaned forward. "Then let me see a woman get out of a headlock with a man."

"Care to volunteer?"

She was feeling so high with physical excitement that she nearly did.

"There's no one better qualified?" she asked.

"There's no one else with doubts like yours."

Stefanie stood up, straightened the top of her running outfit, and approached Dan and Mike. Slowly they showed her the basics of escaping from a headlock. A simple combination of hip swing and blow to the groin, so easy as to seem almost ridiculous.

"Ready?"

"I suppose."

He stepped behind her. Everyone's eyes were riveted on them.

"I feel like there should be a spotlight on us," she muttered as Dan stepped behind her.

Swing hip, drop arm, bring fist to groin. She repeated the procedure silently as Dan explained the technique they would demonstrate to the class. Her heart was fluttering in her throat and she wondered if he would be able to feel it.

"Ready?" His breath ruffled the hair against her cheek.

"Ready."

His arm dug into her throat, pressed against her collarbone. Swing hip—what? She couldn't think. The pressure increased. Her arms fell like dropping autumn leaves.

"Stefanie?" His voice seemed far away, lost in the buzzing sound that roared inside her head. "Move your hips left."

His hand pressed against her spine to move her left. The pressure was gentle, nonthreatening, but the memories exploded with a rush of remembered violence. She was suddenly back in that parking lot, crouched behind the wheel of a rented car, sure she was about to die. She had to get out of there.

She pulled away from him and, bile rising to her throat, ran from the room, the swinging door waving behind her like a flag of surrender.

7

If he hadn't been so mesmerized by the scent of her perfume, Dan might have detected the light film of sweat that had beaded her forehead, the trembling of her hands when she gripped the arm he had pressed against her throat. But, as it was, he had been dizzy with pleasure at her nearness and had allowed the clues he would have noticed immediately in another student to slip by unnoticed.

Now what he wanted most was to protect her from embarrassment.

Calmly, as if nothing unusual had happened, he asked Mike to continue the class, called another student up for the demonstration, then slipped out of the *dojo* and into the hallway. He stood quietly, listening, but the only sound was the soft buzz of the fluorescent light fixture overhead.

"Damn!"

He raced into his office, grabbed the keys for his Porsche from the top of his desk, and was about to go out to look for her when he heard a sound from the ladies' room. He stood in the center of the hallway again, waiting for the sound to return. There. Muffled, low, a soft rustling. He went to the door of the bathroom.

He knocked, a series of three sharp raps on the wooden door.

No answer. Then the sound of water running.

He knocked again.

"A minute. I'm sorry—a minute, please."

He could barely hear her; her voice sounded strained, hoarse.

"Stefanie? Are you all right?"

No answer.

He hesitated no longer than a heartbeat.

"I'm coming in," he said, then opened the door.

She was sitting on the blue tile floor, her head tilted back against the door to the stall. The skin around her eyes seemed smudged a deep purple in contrast to the sudden grayness of her complexion.

A million questions hammered inside his head but he pushed them away. Instead he knelt down beside her and cradled her head against his chest. He had almost expected the fiery waves of her hair to singe his skin wherever they touched him, but instead it was soft and surprisingly cool beneath his fingers.

She burrowed her face more closely against him; her breath tickled his chest. A sudden sparking of desire flared deep inside his belly, but for the first time he could remember in his adult life, it was overshadowed by a swelling of tenderness.

"It's all right," he said, putting an arm around her shivering body. "You're safe now."

"No," she answered. "You're never safe."

"You're wrong." His grip on her shoulders deepened. "You're safe here with me."

He hadn't expected the fineness of her bone structure or the softness of her skin against his chest. At work, dressed in her business clothes, her shoulders seemed straight and strong. However, beneath his hands, the delicacy of her frame made him feel incredibly protective. He breathed deeply and her perfume dizzied his senses for a moment. His pulse had accelerated and he wondered if she could hear his heart beating against her cheek.

"Do you want to talk about it?"

She shook her head, her wavy hair brushing against his skin.

"Not now," she said. "Just hold me, please."

Those four simple words tore into his heart with the precision of a laser beam. They burned through years of accumulated pains and exposed the soft core he tried so hard to hide.

Just hold me.

They were the words his brother Michael had said the night he died. They were the words Michael had uttered in the antiseptic whiteness of the ambulance as it wailed through the cold, cold Boston streets. Dan hadn't heard those words himself; he hadn't been there when Michael needed him. They had been spoken to the emergency technician who had held Michael's hand at the end.

He pulled her closer. He willed his strength to enter her mind, willed his power to aid her, willed his love to keep her safe.

He had no idea how long they sat there on the hard, cold tiles. The minutes bent and twisted around him, unreal as ghosts and spirits. Outside students chattered as they moved through the hallway toward the dressing room. Someone knocked on the locked bathroom door.

"Sorry," he called out in a voice that was light and easy. "We're having a few plumbing problems. Use the men's room, okay?"

The footsteps receded.

He wanted everyone to leave, everyone but Stefanie. He was a willing captive, glad to spend the rest of the night with her close to his heart.

However, the laughing and chatting of the students as they passed the bathroom door had brought her out of her malaise. She sat up and brushed her hair off her face with quick, sharp gestures.

"I apologize for taking you away from the class like that, Dan."

"You didn't take me away. I chose to leave."

"You wouldn't have had to make that choice if I hadn't bolted. I'm sorry."

She stood up and straightened the top of her running outfit, brushing away a few pieces of lint from her pants. He stood up next to her. She glanced into the mirror over the sink.

"I look like death." She placed her hands on her cheeks, staring at the pale woman reflected back at her.

He ignored the comment. "I'm willing to listen if you'd like to talk," he said, watching her in the mirror's surface.

A small smile lit her face as she glanced around the utilitarian bathroom. "I don't really think this is the place."

He felt himself redden. "In my office then. Over coffee."

"Make everything right with coffee, huh?" Her smile brightened. "Give me a few moments to resurrect myself and I'll join you, okay?"

She waited until the door closed behind him, then let herself sag against the sink. Drops of water on the edge spotted her running pants. The acrid taste of bile still lay against her tongue and she longed to brush her teeth. Instead, she washed her face, stripping it of the residue of makeup. Then she rinsed her mouth, dried her skin, and stepped from the brightly lit bathroom into the dim hallway.

She could hear him rustling around in his office at the end of the corridor. For a second she toyed with the idea of grabbing her car keys and disappearing, but, no. It wouldn't be fair to Dan and, even more important, it wouldn't be fair to her.

"Cream and sugar?" Dan's voice echoed through the long hallway.

She straightened her shoulders and walked toward his office.

"Sounds perfect."

Dan, holding two mugs of coffee, turned at the sound of her voice in the doorway. He handed her one. "Not custom blend, I'm afraid," he said, nodding toward the big jar of instant on his metal desk.

"We seem to be establishing a tradition of bad coffee."

"There are worse traditions."

She sipped the coffee then rolled her eyes.

"I'm not so sure about that."

Stefanie fiddled with her spoon, twirling it around and around in the mug while Dan watched her, waiting.

Finally she spoke.

"I suppose an explanation is in order," she began, putting her cup down on his desk.

"It's not a requirement," he said, "but if you'd like to talk, I'm here."

She crossed her arms around her chest. The office seemed very cold and suddenly very large.

He motioned for her to sit on the black sofa near the window. "You'll be more comfortable."

She shook her head. "No, thanks." Outside the wind rustled against the window frame and she shivered. All of the students had left and she felt as if she'd been dropped into a strange country. "Listen, if you don't mind, I think maybe I'd better go home instead. I must be keeping you from something."

"You haven't finished your coffee."

She picked up the white mug, took two large sips, then placed it back down on his desk. "I appreciate your trouble, but I really should get going."

He walked toward her, his long legs eating up the floor with two strides. His eyes rested on her arms-across-the-chest pose and she forced her limbs to fall loosely to her sides.

She smiled at him. "Better?"

"Much."

He longed to reach out and touch her hair, to imprint the scent and touch of her once again on his brain, but he knew it wasn't the time.

"You were ready to talk, Stefanie. Why the change of heart?"

She hesitated a moment, trying to think of an excuse—laundry left undone, a phone call she needed to make—some useful social lie to cover her pain. In the end, though, her honesty won out.

"The truth is I'm suddenly feeling a bit awkward and more than a little embarrassed." She reached out to him and rested her hand on his forearm. "Can you understand?"

He thought of the people who had passed through his school. He understood better than she knew.

He cleared his throat.

"I understand. But one thing I don't understand is what I did wrong in there."

"You did nothing wrong. It's just when your arm went around my throat—well, it brought back a lot of things I'd rather..." Her voice faded off. "You know."

He stepped closer to her and let his hand rest on top of her red hair.

"I don't know," he said, his voice softer than she would have imagined possible, "but I want to. I want to know all about you."

A sweet pain pierced through her and rendered her speechless for a moment. It was as if her ribs had cracked open to accommodate her growing heart.

"No one knows all about me," she managed at last.

"Then let me be the first." His fingers on her cheek were lightly caressing. "Let's go somewhere and talk."

She shook her head. "I don't think I could stand a crowd tonight. If you don't mind, I'd rather we go to my apartment. I would rather be home tonight."

"You'd feel comfortable with me there?"

"I'd feel very comfortable with you there."

She smiled at him and his heart soared.

Dan had to stay and lock up the school so Stefanie drew him a map to her apartment. She was glad to have time to do some last-minute straightening up. Leading the solitary life she did, she was often less than careful about putting things in order. Her cleaning woman wasn't due until Thursday and she needed to be sure no stray lingerie or other equally embarrassing item was visible.

She made good time and quickly got the apartment into decent shape. She also managed to find time to reapply her makeup, fluff up her hair, and change into a close-fitting pair of jeans and her favorite over-sized gold cashmere sweater. She was in the middle of adjusting the sofa pillows for the third time when the front doorbell chimed.

She peered through the peephole, then undid the metal tangle of locks and chains that she'd had installed a few months ago.

"Hi. Come on in."

Dan stepped into the tiny foyer and slipped off his jacket, looking as awkward as she felt. She hung it in the hall closet.

"You should have asked who was out there before you opened the door, Stefanie."

She grinned and pointed toward the security peephole. "I made a visual ID, Mr. O'Connor."

He looked at the door and nodded. "You can't be too careful."

"So I've heard."

She led him into her living room and motioned him to the sofa against the long wall.

"Coffee? A drink?"

"Scotch, if you have it."

She nodded and walked over to the bar near the stereo system.

"Straight? On the rocks?"

"Straight."

While she was rummaging around, trying to remember if Johnnie Walker Red was better than Dewar's, Dan got up and walked round the small living room, looking at the metal and glass furniture, the stark draperies, the anonymous prints on the pale gold walls.

She handed him the drink. "Is there something wrong?"

He took a swallow and sat back down on the couch. "Sorry. It's just this place—it's nothing like I imagined your home would be."

She sat down on the edge of a small black-and-white chair and smiled at him. "What did you think my home would be like?"

"More like you, I suppose. More feminine. This is asexual."

She sipped the club soda she'd poured for herself before he arrived. "You're pretty observant. This is a furnished place."

He nodded. "Thought so. You'd never have stuff like this."

"Really? What would I have?" She was beginning to enjoy this.

He shot her a quick look, then, reassured by her twinkling eyes, he continued. "Family photos, a big piano, lots of books, a cat in a rocking chair—you know."

"Sounds like the little old lady who lived in a shoe," she said, laughing.

He loved the sound of her laugh, full and throaty. A woman's laugh.

"A little old lady? No way. You're just a very feminine woman and I expected your apartment to be like you—beautiful."

She turned as red as the accent pillow in the corner of the sofa.

"With my job there's no time to decorate an apartment. I barely have time to unpack before Tele-Com has me on the road again. This is the longest I've been in one place since I began working for them."

Suddenly the Scotch seemed to be burning a hole in his stomach.

"How long have you been on the island?"

"It'll be two years in December when my contract's up."

He could barely force the next question out.

"What then? Will you stay here?"

There was no simple answer to his question so she chose to sidestep it.

"Can I freshen your drink?" She stood up and motioned toward the bar.

"Thanks, no." He patted the seat next to him on the sofa. "But you could sit down next to me. Please?"

She took her drink over to the couch and sat on the end cushion, far enough away so she couldn't catch the scent of his cologne or feel the heat of his body. So she could think.

"So," she said, tucking her legs beneath her, "you've come to hear the saga of Stefanie Colt."

He leaned toward her. "If you want to tell it."

She turned her hands palm upward. "You've probably heard the same story in all its variations, Dan. Crimes are committed every day, everywhere—I happened to find mine a few months ago on a business trip."

"In the city?" A combination of anger and fear began to push against his chest.

"No." She laughed grimly. "In Council Bluffs, Iowa. Can you imagine that? Here I am living in New York and I managed to get mugged in Iowa, of all damned places. I didn't know they *had* crime in Iowa, for heaven's sake."

"We don't have the market cornered, you know."

"So I found out."

He touched her wrist and her breath caught.

"Tell me."

Those dark eyes were fixed on her. There was something about them, a strange kind of magnetism that seemed to draw the words from her throat before she had the chance to censor them, to make them prettier.

"I have to travel a lot for my job," she began, picking at the sleeve of her sweater with one long fingernail. "It was one of the things that originally attracted me to Tele-Com. Sitting at a desk was no big thrill but the allure of travel was too seductive for me to resist."

She explained how she'd gotten used to the late nights in strange cities, learning the intricacies of parkways and freeways and interstates, juggling foreign currency and strange tongues. For the first few years it was great fun, almost compensation for what had proved to be a rather dull job beneath the glitzy surface.

"Conway has a regional office in Omaha," she said, meeting his eyes for the first time since she began to speak, "and we had just installed some new equipment in it and were holding an orientation workshop just before Easter." She shook her head and scraped her red hair off her face as she spoke. "I'd traveled enough to know that even the Pope would have a tough time getting a seat just before Easter, so I called one of those little commuter services that fly out of MacArthur Airport in Bohemia."

Dan nodded. Many business people had started to use the smaller airport on mid-Long Island rather than the busier and less accessible La Guardia and JFK in Queens.

She took another sip of club soda. As she spoke, he noticed her voice was growing calmer, almost as if the very act of telling her story was shining light on the dark corridors of her fear.

"I worked it out so I took a small ten-seater from here to Philly. From there I took People Express to Detroit and from Detroit I switched back to another small plane that took me into Eppley in Omaha."

"Omaha is west of Iowa. Where does Council Bluffs fit into this?"

She touched his forearm for a second.

"I'll explain. Omaha is a curious town. It's one of the larger cities in that part of the country but it doesn't have its own airport. Eppley Field is actually just over the state line in Council Bluffs, Iowa. So when you fly to Omaha, you get two states for the price of one."

"Very economical."

"You'd almost think they were New Englanders, wouldn't you?"

She drained her glass, then noticed that Dan had finished his Scotch.

"I'm getting a little more. Care for a refill?"

He shook his head.

"Just some of your club soda. I still have to drive home."

Moments later she took her place back on the sofa, her legs once more curled beneath her body. Her toes were polished a pale peach color and he found himself amazingly distracted by such a normally uninteresting part of the human anatomy.

"Anyway, I landed in Iowa around one in the morning. My business meeting was just seven hours away and I wanted nothing more than to get into town and get some rest. The rental car company we used was situated at the far end of the field. At that hour no shuttle buses were available but—this was Iowa, wasn't it?" Her voice had taken on an ironic tone. "Surely I could walk a quarter-mile to get my car."

A sense of urgency rocketed through him and he wanted to shake her, to make her spill out the story faster and faster until it was just a tiny speck of nothing on the horizon, until she was far past it. However, he knew the pace was hers.

"Could you?"

She shook her head. "No, I couldn't." She put her glass down on the octagonal table in front of the couch. "You know, I nearly made it, too." She held up her hand, her thumb and index finger a mere inch apart. "I was this close to the office when it—" She stopped, some of the cool self-possession that marked her speech failing her as she covered her eyes.

His gut twisted.

"Were you raped, Stefanie?"

It was the hardest question he'd ever asked and, as he waited for her answer, he felt himself suspended over flame.

"Thank God, no."

The flames receded but he could still feel the heat.

"I couldn't have lived through something like that," she said.

Dan took her hand, pressed it between his own. "You would live through whatever you had to. You're stronger than you know."

"Really?" She arched an eyebrow. "You wouldn't think that if you'd seen me that night."

He could feel the tension in her hand and he released it. She was the kind of woman who had to hold her pain privately. Strength was written in her face, in the finely hewn bones of her jaw and cheek. A vision of her, cowed and bruised, flashed jaggedly across his brain and he found the sight obscene.

She sketched in the details briefly, with as little emotion attached to them as possible. An arm across her throat, a gun pressed against her spine, the coiling grasping fear that sucked air from her lungs and rational thought from her brain; the unspeakable notion that life could be over so quickly.

"I kept thinking, 'Not here, not here.' It seemed so ludicrous somehow to die next to the wheel of a 1983 Chevette. I mean"—she managed a small laugh—"a Cadillac maybe, but what on earth would my family say about a Chevette?"

He smiled with her but filed her remark about her family away for future reference. He brought the subject back on target.

"How badly were you hurt?" He hadn't noticed any scars, any lingering physical aftereffects.

"Nothing too terrible," she answered. "A black eye and two broken ribs. Nothing that a little makeup and shallow breathing couldn't remedy."

"And?"

Stefanie looked at him, weighing him with her gaze, taking measure of something innately immeasurable.

"And the physical is only a small part of the damage." She tilted her head slightly to the left. "But you knew that, didn't you?"

He nodded.

She closed her eyes and rested her head back against the wall behind the sofa.

"I've never been one for irony, but even I can't avoid the black humor in this situation. That man committed the crime, but I'm the one serving the sentence. Funny, isn't it?"

"No." His voice was hard and angry. "Not funny at all."

She finished her second glass of club soda and he got up and poured her another one. She nodded her thanks when he brought it back to her. She was feeling a slight buzzing inside her head not unlike what she used to experience when she drank too much wine. But she hadn't had any alcohol since developing an ulcer.

He sat back down on the couch next to her. They still weren't near enough to touch. She didn't need to touch him. Blame it on nerves, blame it on his nearness, but she felt they were communicating on a level deeper than the spoken word.

"Well, *Sensei,* is there hope for me?"

She tried to sound light and breezy, but she fooled neither Dan nor herself. She dropped the pose. "I'm tired of being frightened. I'm tired of feeling weak and vulnerable. I want to feel I'm in control of my life again." She thought of her job and all of her dissatisfactions."

"That's a pretty tall order, Ms. Colt."

The corners of her mouth tilted up in a smile of such sweetness and trust that he felt privileged to be its object.

"But I thought you were the purveyor of magic, the granter of wishes, the—"

He threw his head back and laughed, a deep full sound of pure pleasure.

"Hold up, Stefanie!" He gathered her hands and held them for a moment. "*Sensei* means teacher, not wizard."

How could she explain to him her certainty that he was capable of magic?

"Then what?" she asked. "I doubt you'd let me back into class after my display tonight. Magic was my only hope."

He made an expression of annoyance.

"If you want to rejoin the class, I'd welcome you."

She drew a deep breath.

"I'll be honest with you, Dan—I think I'd prefer private lessons, if you would."

"No."

"No?"

"No."

"Why not?" She thought he was kidding, although the stern look on his face gave her pause. "I'd be very embarrassed to go back in that class."

His blue eyes darkened even more. "Good."

"Good?" She was beginning to sound like a parrot. She leaped to her feet. "I don't understand you at all. One moment you're the most compassionate man I've ever met, and the next you're acting like a total—" She hesitated.

"Bastard?" His eyes twinkled. If he laughed, she was afraid she'd throw her shoe at him.

"Yes," she said, glaring at him. "A bastard. If it's a question of money, I'd be glad to pay you the going rate."

That did it. The twinkle was extinguished.

"Ah, yes," he said. "Money. The great equalizer, the cornerstone of American democracy."

Stefanie threw her hands up in disgust.

"Then, why not? If it's not a question of money—"

Dan jumped to his feet and faced her over the coffee table. "You want it easy, don't you, lady? You want a nice neat package all wrapped up in dollar bills. Well, you've got the wrong man for that. I'm not gonna make it easy for you, Colt. No way."

For a moment she felt dangerously close to tears. Anger and some unnamed emotion brought her heart closer to the surface.

"I never said I want it easy, Dan."

He caught the slight tremble in her voice and moved quickly around the table to be next to her. All his life passion had tended to take the sound and form of anger, frightening the people he cared most about.

"You're right. You never did." It was his preconceptions that colored her words. "If you want private lessons, I can give them to you, Stefanie. But I don't think it would be fair to you."

Her anger ebbed as quickly as it had first flowed. She waited for him to continue, her rage being replaced by excitement at his closeness and pleasure at his concern.

"I don't want you to be comfortable in class," he continued. "I don't want you to feel at ease or sure of yourself."

Her eyes widened. "You want me nervous?"

He moved a step closer. She wanted to step back but forced herself to hold her ground.

"I want you to be intimidated."

She found her voice. "Like now?"

He grinned down at her. "Like now."

A broad smile broke across her face. "You imitate the uncertainties of life in your class?"

"See what an education can do?" He grinned and the tension in her shoulders disappeared. "Care to write my advertising copy for me?"

She knew her own eyes sparkled now. "Ask me again in a couple of weeks. I never endorse an untried product."

"You'll come back to class?"

She nodded. "I'm ready for it, Dan. I want to run my own life, not be run over by it."

He put his hand on her shoulder. "You won't regret it."

"I know I won't."

The atmosphere had changed without them realizing it. It was a subtle alteration, a gentle swaying of their bodies toward one another, an awareness of scents, of possibilities.

His arms went gently around her. He didn't draw her closer and neither did she move closer on her own.

"I know it's too soon," he said, his breath smelling slightly of Scotch.

"Yes," she said, not altogether sure that it was. His fingers played against her spine and she felt her mind race with fantasies.

"It won't always be too soon, though. I want you to understand my intentions."

Her smile was a mystical combination of sexy and shy and he longed to take her right there, right on that sharp-edged sofa of hers.

"Dishonorable, *Sensei?*"

Her eyes grew heavy-lidded with a desire that matched his.

"Definitely dishonorable."

Stefanie watched his mouth form his words as if she were watching a wonderful movie. He looked deliciously evil, marvelously threatening. More than anything, she wanted that mouth on hers.

"I'm glad," she said. "You would disappoint me otherwise."

He moved a fraction closer. Her breath stopped for a moment.

"I'll never disappoint you." His voice was a rough caress.

The moment became unbearably sweet, laced with erotic vibrations that made her skin tingle. She could imagine the softness of his beard against her cheek, she knew how that mouth would feel on hers, knew how her body would respond, was already responding even without those stimuli.

She lifted her head for his kiss.

Instead, he cupped her chin with one large hand, sliding his fingers across the firm line of her jaw.

"I have a rule," he said. "No teacher-student relationships."

She nuzzled her chin against his hand like a kitten seeking tactile pleasure.

"No exceptions?"

"None so far."

She smiled and stepped away from him, feeling powerful and strong. "Then, so be it, *Sensei*. I bow to your greater will."

She got his leather jacket from her closet and handed it to him. He shrugged into it and she led him to the door.

Dan gave her information about the next class, told her where she could buy a *gi*. She gave him her home phone number and thanked him for his help that evening.

She unbolted and unchained the door to let him out.

But just before he disappeared down the stairwell, he turned back toward her.

"Four more weeks, Stefanie. Then there are no rules at all."

8

"Got a minute, Colt?"

Stefanie looked up from the cost forecast for Tele-Com that she was working on for the end-of-month review and saw Gabe, shirt-sleeves rolled up, glasses askew, standing in the doorway to her office.

"For you, Gabe, always. Come on in."

Never light on his feet, Gabe Freeman's step was heavier than usual as he crossed the small office and slumped into the leather chair near her desk.

"How do you do it?" he asked, removing his glasses and rubbing the bridge of his nose. "Are you taking illegal substances or what?"

"How do I do what?" she countered.

"Get so damned much done every day. You're running all over this building nonstop—no one can catch up with you. I get tired just watching you."

She grinned and shrugged her shoulders. "You know the saying—the more you do, the more you do."

"Big help you are," he said, scowling into the bright autumn sun streaming in her office window. "Advice like that I can get from a fortune cookie."

"Is the baby keeping you up nights?"

He shook his head. "No. That's quieted down for now. Eileen says we have a few months' peace until the teething begins."

She felt a quick stab of envy. "Ahh," she said, laughing. "Poor daddy."

He grinned good-naturedly. "I'm doing a lot of complaining, aren't I?" he asked.

She grinned back. "No more than usual. Now, what can I do for you?"

"Oh, yeah—it felt so good sitting here I nearly forgot why I came in." He rummaged around in his shirt pocket and pulled out a folded piece of paper. "Your brother Brenda called—"

She laughed out loud. "Brendan, Gabe. Brendan."

He just shrugged. "Brendan. I just figured you Colts had a skeleton or two in your family closet."

"Very funny." She was smiling as she said it. "What did he want?"

"He didn't say. He just left the message that he called and a number."

He handed her the paper and she squinted at the marks. "Hieroglyphics?"

"Runes, wise guy." He took it back from her, stared at it for a few moments, then turned beet-red. "Sorry. I can't read this thing either."

He looked so embarrassed that she dropped her teasing tone.

"Don't worry, Gabe. He'll call back if it's important. He probably just had a little family gossip for me."

Gabe pulled a cigarette out of his pocket, but, at Stefanie's frown, stuck it right back in.

"Did old man Conway see you about the Denver trip?"

"Denver?" Her ulcer began to bother her.

Gabe muttered a mild expletive. "He was supposed to set it up with you and Tele-Com for next week."

She lowered her head and massaged a spot on her rib cage.

"Stef?"

She looked up."

"Are you all right?"

"Of course," she answered. "I just have the beginnings of an ulcer flare-up."

He pulled a foil-wrapped package of Maalox from his back pocket. "Here. Take two. They work for me."

She shook her head. "Is there anything you don't have in those pockets, for heaven's sake?"

"Early Boy Scout training," he said, "but don't change the subject." He leaned forward, elbows on thighs. "They're beginning to notice, you know."

"Notice what?" The pain in her side deepened, burning intense against her ribs.

"You haven't made a field trip since March."

"April."

"It's still a long time ago, Stefanie. Too long. The old man is beginning to rumble."

"Let him. He's not my boss. I answer to Tele-Com."

"Stefanie—"

"I appreciate your concern, Gabe," she said, standing up and walking around to the other side of her desk, "but my contract is up in a few months. If they don't like the way I've been handling things around here, they can just let me go."

He looked at her for a moment, then shook his head. "Of course. Why didn't I see it? You're afraid to fly!"

"Gabe, really—that's not it."

He stood up, too, and faced her.

"Then, what? You've been the best rep we've ever had here. I'd hate to see you quit over something as stupid as a trip to Denver." He stopped and looked at her with sad brown eyes. "I like to think we're more than business associates, Stef. I think of you as a friend. Believe it or not, I'm a good listener."

She patted his arm. "I know you are, Gabriel. It's just there's nothing much to listen to. Maybe I'm approaching a midlife crisis."

"Try that one again in ten years, Colt. I won't buy it now." He jammed his hands in the pockets of his baggy khaki pants. "Even though we have ways to make you talk, I'll drop it for now."

She smiled. "Too many late-night movies, Freeman."

After Gabe left, she got up, closed the door to her office, then slipped out of her shoes. Unbuttoning the top button of her gray plaid skirt, she began to do a series of stretching and breathing exercises Dan had taught her that she found did wonders for alleviating a day's accumulated stresses and strains.

Dan inspired confidence and she had also discovered that he was as good as his word.

Stefanie was already two-and-a-half weeks into the self-defense course and not once had he stepped away from his role as the *sensei* to become Dan. If it hadn't been for the way his dark blue eyes sometimes lingered on her for a moment longer than necessary or the way he watched her from the window of his office each night as she crossed the parking lot to her car, she would have been convinced she had imagined everything.

Although she hated to admit it, she was grateful in a way that he was keeping his word. She hadn't expected the experience of taking a self-defense course to be so sexually charged and, if he had chosen to bridge the gap between them, she wasn't sure how she would respond. No. That was a lie. She knew exactly how she would respond and she wasn't ready for that yet.

There was such a thing as getting to know one another, finding out about the man who was now privy to such personal matters about her while she knew nothing about him, not even the most basic biographical details.

The specter of the Hawaii trip in November, coupled with the Denver business, tugged at the edges of her mind, but she was finally gaining some perspective about it. Perhaps there was more than a metaphorical "fear of flying" at work here. Perhaps she was beginning to resent the demands her job made on their personal life, or on what personal life she had. And, just maybe, the assault, as terrifying as it had been, was a catalyst impelling her to reexamine her life and its direction.

By the time she finished her exercises, she no longer felt the twinging pain of her ulcer. She rebuttoned the waistband of her skirt, slipped her shoes back on, and took her seat behind her desk, ready to tackle business once again. The rest of the day slid by quickly.

By six o'clock she was ready to lock the office door behind her and head for class. Brendan hadn't called again and, with all apologies to her twin brother, there wasn't very much in heaven or on earth that could make her miss an opportunity to watch Dan weave his magic.

"Stefanie? Can you stay a moment?"

She was about to go into the dressing room to slip out of her *gi* and back into her business clothes when his voice caught her in midstride. One of the other students, a tall blonde, turned to her.

"Lucky you. *Sensei* never asked me to stay after class."

Stefanie said nothing. She merely smiled at the woman, her well-practiced Yankee caution firmly in place. What had just moments ago been a noisy studio filled with women of all ages struggling to learn the intricacies of self-defense was now a silent room except for the hum of the air conditioner in the corner.

Dan's back was to her. He stood on the other side of the *dojo,* bending over a young man who had stayed on after early class to help Dan demonstrate a few techniques that night. His feet were wide apart in his characteristic stance, knees slightly bent. A white sweatband kept some of his curly dark hair off his face. She could see where some of the curls were damp from perspiration as she crossed the room toward him.

"Thanks, Jimmy," he was saying as she neared the two men. "I'll see you tomorrow."

Jimmy bent over in the reflexive bow common to the art, then left the room. She waited, silent and slightly uneasy, for Dan to say something. Instead he busied himself putting away the mats they had used, whistling a small, unidentifiable tune. She heard the outer door swing open and close a few times as students left for the night.

Finally she cleared her throat. "Dan? You wanted to see me?" She didn't sound like herself; her voice was thin and tight with tension.

He locked the supply closet and turned toward her. For a split second she could see an oddly vulnerable look in his eyes and her heart turned over inside her chest.

"How did you like class tonight?" he asked, yanking off the sweatband and running his hands through his hair.

"Excellent, Dan. Really."

What was the matter with her? Why did she sound like she was giving a speech in front of a group of mourners? There must be some middle ground between this absurdly formal response and the urge that raced through her to say that his raw power, chained by his mind and tempered by his sensitivity, had been unbearably erotic to her.

When she was supposed to be concentrating on blocking and punching, sudden unexpected visions of tangled sheets and rumpled blankets, of long and passionate bouts of lovemaking flashed across her mind like lightning during a storm. She wrapped her arms securely across her middle, stroking the white sash on her *gi*.

"No feedback?" Those darkly magnetic eyes of his burned through her, incinerating her defenses with the speed and accuracy of a laser beam.

"No suggestions?" he continued. "You're a good businesswoman, Stefanie. I'd value your opinion."

Unfair, she thought. *Unfair to soften me with praise.*

"Well," she said slowly, feeling her way, "I do think you should make a videotape of your sales presentation. It could be a marvelous tool for reaching more of the Long Island business community."

He nodded. While she was speaking, he had moved a step closer to her and she caught the faint scent of salt and spice.

"What about taping one of my classes at Conway?" A faint smile played at the right corner of his mouth.

"Too large," she answered, her voice clearer and more certain now that they were on familiar ground. "You have to choreograph a small group to get the effect you need. There can't be any wasted words or wasted motion—everything has to be zeroed in on the goal."

His eyes drifted pointedly down to her mouth. Her bright lipstick had faded, emphasizing the fullness of her lips. She talked animatedly as they crossed the *dojo* to the door. When she spoke about business she lost that slightly frightened look that had haunted him since the day on the ferry. He wanted to be the one to erase that look forever, to make her come alive beneath his hands the same way he came alive whenever she was in the room.

He switched off the light and reached for her hand to guide her the last few feet through the darkness to the staircase. When he touched her, a spark jumped between them, arcing silver in the blackened room.

She chuckled softly. "Static electricity," she said in her relentlessly logical way.

"Don't be so sure," he answered. "I think it was man-made."

"You're a romantic, *Sensei?*" she murmured as she placed the palm of her hand unerringly on the bared and warm expanse of skin on his chest.

"You inspire dreams."

The tension between them was exquisite. She couldn't see his eyes, had no visual signal to tell her what would happen next. The only realities were the mingled perfumes of their skin, the fluttering of her pulse, and the answering pounding of his heart beneath her hand. Moving simultaneously, they drew closer until her breasts, covered by the thin cotton outfit, grazed his chest. She could feel her power over him by the way his breath caught loud and ragged in his throat. And, with the way her body yielded like a pool of molten gold, she silently acknowledged his power over her.

Her lips parted slightly in anticipation and he lowered his head closer to hers and was about to kiss her and—

"The door was unlocked." The voice was definitely familiar as it floated in from the entrance hall. "Is anybody here?"

"Brendan," she breathed, desire being replaced by a combination of embarrassment and annoyance.

Dan dropped her arms as if they had suddenly caught fire.

"Brendan?" His voice was as hard as the line of his body.

"My brother," she explained, feeling a burst of pleasure at his display of jealousy.

"Is his timing always this good?"

Stefanie chuckled, remembering the times Brendan would manage to pop out of the house just as a date was about to kiss her good night in the driveway.

"Yes," she said, smoothing back her hair as Dan led her up the four steps toward the entrance hall. "I'm afraid it always is."

Brendan's back was to them as they came down the hallway and she noticed the expensive lines of his suit and the paradoxical shaggy hair and running shoes. Katie's influence was far-reaching.

He turned as they stepped onto the tile floor of the lobby. His eyes flickered from Dan to Stefanie then back to Dan.

Don't say anything, she thought, praying his twin-radar was working. *This is too important for jokes.*

Brendan extended his hand and the two men shook hands.

"I'm Brendan Colt," he said, his grin much like his sister's. "Stefanie's brother."

"Dan O'Connor." He narrowed his eyes as he looked at the younger man before him. "I'd know you two were related anywhere."

Brendan's face bore the same patrician stamp in the pronounced cheekbones and firm jaw, albeit in a more masculine delineation, that Stefanie's carried. She embraced her brother and affectionately ruffled his hair.

"Actually Bren forgot to tell you he's my younger brother," she teased.

Dan arched an eyebrow. "Younger? You two look enough alike to be twins."

Brendan shot her a look of brotherly annoyance. "We are twins," he explained, smiling at Dan. "She just likes to get in a dig now and then because she's two minutes older than I am."

"Two minutes and thirty-five seconds older," Stefanie elaborated. "Just in the interests of accuracy, you understand."

There was a brief, slightly uncomfortable silence. Dan hooked his fingers in his black belt and stood, feet apart, waiting for some clue as to what was next. Stefanie felt her nerves begin to jangle alarmingly. She knew she had to say something, but her senses were still so filled with Dan and their interlude in the darkened room that she found her mind unable to form the words of easy conversation. Besides, there was the genuine discomfort of knowing that, of all people in the world, Brendan was the one who would pick up on exactly what she was feeling.

She was right.

They hadn't been making love, of that Brendan was sure. However, there was a look in Stefanie's eyes he had never seen before. It was almost as if an invisible veil had been lifted and he was able to see inside her mind. And the slightly sharp angles of her face and body seemed more rounded, their edges gently curved and softened with—what? Passion? Love? Brendan caught her eyes and in the flickering of an instant he knew where he had seen that look before.

His mirror.

When he fell in love with Katie.

"Brendan? Did you hear me?" Stefanie's voice brought him back to here and now. He looked at her again. "How on earth did you find out where I was?"

He smiled at her and Dan. "I dropped by your office around seven thirty and your pal, Gabe Freeman, told me you were at class. I didn't know you were interested in karate."

"Not karate," Dan said, rolling his "r's" in true Japanese fashion. "Stefanie's learning a self-defense technique based on the mother art of jujitsu."

She stared at him. "I am?" she asked in honest surprise. "All this time I thought I was learning karate. How come you never explained that to me?"

Dan laughed. "You never asked."

Brendan's eyes narrowed. "Why the sudden interest in self-defense, Red? Is there anything I should know about?"

She shook her head. "In case you haven't heard, it's a cold world out there. A woman can't be too careful."

Something didn't feel right to Brendan. Over the past few months he'd had the occasional sense that all wasn't right with his sister, but the wonder of falling in love had kept his unease relegated to a corner of his brain.

He cleared his throat. "Listen—I'm in need of an emergency fix of food. Why don't you both join me? Maybe we can find a restaurant around here that's still open."

Stefanie glanced at Dan, not wanting to push him into anything. "If you have something you'd rather do, I understand..." she began.

Dan, however, was all in favor of the idea. "There's a terrific little Mom-and-Pop Italian restaurant in a shopping center along Jericho Turnpike in Elwood. Give us five minutes to change and we'll go."

"Do they have eggplant rollatini?" Brendan asked.

"Best on the island," Dan answered.

"Then you've got a deal." He turned to his sister, who was staring at the two men who had just decided her evening for her. "What are you waiting for, Red? Let's get moving!"

Stefanie put down her fork and stared at the empty plate where her shrimp fra diavolo had been.

"That was delicious," she sighed, smiling at Dan. "How on earth did you find this place?"

The restaurant was a tiny storefront operation with mended cloth tablecovers and votive candles on every table, not at all the type of place either she or her brother were used to.

"Word of mouth," Dan answered. "I got sick of those fancy places with the engraved menus and the lousy service."

She blushed as if he'd been able to read her mind.

He ran a hand over the red-and-white checkered cloth and looked at the trailing plants and vines that hung suspended from the ceiling. "This place makes me feel like I'm home again."

"I thought your last name was O'Connor," Brendan said, finishing his eggplant. "I'd expect lace curtains and corned beef and cabbage."

She detected a sharp edge of curiosity in her brother's voice, a not totally pleasant sound. However, she was so curious about Dan's answer that she refrained from gently changing the subject. Maybe she could begin to accumulate some of the pieces to the puzzle Dan was.

"That's on my dad's side," he answered. "My mother was Angelina DiNatale."

"Was?" Stefanie asked.

"She died last year."

Her hand reached out and covered his in a spontaneous gesture of sympathy.

"I'm sorry," she said softly.

"So am I," he answered. "So am I."

Their waitress approached the table and draped an arm over Dan's shoulder.

"Would you and your friends like some dessert, Danny?" she asked, giving a maternal pat to his head. "Our rum cake is the best around."

Dan snapped out of his melancholy mood. He smiled at the older woman. "How about coffee for three and rum cake?"

"Sounds fine," Brendan said, not sounding altogether thrilled to Stefanie's ears.

Paula, balancing their empty plates precariously along the length of her plump arm, hurried back toward the kitchen, pushing the swinging door open with her hip.

"I'm going to have to go on a fruit juice fast after this," Stefanie said with a groan as she pushed her chair back from the table. "I haven't eaten that much in weeks."

"It shows," Brendan said, looking at his sister. "You must have lost ten pounds in the last few months."

Stefanie saw the look Dan gave her and she knew he would understand and not give her away. "When I work hard I don't eat. It's a family trait."

Brendan laughed. "Not anymore. Didn't you see Harrison's paunch back on Labor Day?"

"No, but he had on a suit and I really couldn't tell."

Brendan was about to launch into a description of their older brother's eating habits when Dan stood up.

"Would you two excuse me for a second? I left my plastic in the glove compartment."

His long legs carried him quickly out of the small restaurant. Brendan waited until the door closed behind him before he spoke.

"What's with him? Was it something I said?"

"He left his credit cards in the car," Stefanie answered. "You heard him."

"Yes, I heard him, but I don't believe him. What's with that guy, anyway?"

She looked at her brother, her green eyes trying to penetrate his normally cheerful exterior.

"You're a snob, Brendan. I never realized it before, but you are."

Her brother gave her a look of disgust.

"You don't believe that, Red, and you know it. Wasn't I always the rebel in our family?"

She thought of his escapades as a slightly wild teenager, then she thought about Katie, the woman he loved, who didn't quite fit the Colt family mold. For a second she wondered if that wasn't part of Katie's attraction, but something about the thought was disturbing to her and she pushed it out of her mind.

"Agreed Dan is not a graduate of Harvard," she said, "but he is a success in his field, Brendan."

Her brother tapped his fingers against the side of the table, his glance lingering for a second on the mended spot on the tablecloth near his water glass. "Beards and leather jackets make me nervous," he said finally.

She lifted the edge of the tablecloth and looked at his feet. "Harris Tweed and Adidas are hardly *haute couture,* brother dear."

Paula scurried back to their table, carrying three tiny glasses of Amaretto on a round tray. "On the house," she said with a warm smile, putting them down on the table. "Enjoy."

Brendan sipped his drink but Stephanie left hers untouched. Brendan abruptly put the drink down and pushed the glass away from him. He leaned toward his sister. "How much do you know about him, Stef?"

She stared at him. "As much as I need to at the moment. Why?" His interest was beginning to annoy her. Brendan had been many things in his day but unreasonable and snobbish were never among them.

"Are you two involved?"

"That's none of your business, Brendan." Her tone was glacial.

He softened. "Look, Red, I'm not trying to do a family number on you."

"You could have fooled me." She knew her brother very well and understood the surges of minor jealousy and protectiveness that ebbed and flowed. Still, his fraternal warning rankled.

"He's a tough character," Brendan continued. "Look at him. Listen to him. You may be out of your league this time, Red."

"Thanks for your vote of confidence." Her voice had risen and she forced herself to lower it to the decibel level of polite conversation. "I'm a grown woman, Brendan—I'm not trying to upstage you. But I do know a few things about life. I haven't been living in a convent for twenty-eight years."

He put his hands over his ears in a playful gesture. "Quiet! I don't want my illusions about my sister shattered."

She relaxed a little. "Don't judge Dan by what you see, please, Bren. Give him the same chance you wanted us to give Katie." She thought about the extreme tenderness Dan had shown her the night she cried. "Let me do this on my own. It's a little late in life to become the protective brother."

He relented. "Just do yourself a favor and don't bring him along next month for the family dinner. Katie is about as much middle class as they can handle."

The very thought of Dan, complete with leather jacket, at her parent's dinner table, made her giggle.

"Could you imagine their faces when they see Dan's beard?" she asked with a laugh.

"What about Dan's beard?"

They both jumped in surprise at the sound of Dan's other-side-of-town voice near them.

Stefanie flushed but it wasn't visible in the dim light of the restaurant. "We—umm—we were just talking about how some people don't trust men with beards."

Dan sat down and put his napkin on his lap.

"If you think that's bad, you should have seen me years ago when I wore an earring."

"An earring?" Stefanie's voice had risen an octave. Her brother shot her an "I-told-you-so" look.

Dan's eyes twinkled. "Just a small one," he said, obviously relishing their shock. "Back in my Hollywood days."

"Hollywood?" Brendan's voice had lost some of that "overseer" tone he'd had moments ago. "Did you teach self-defense in Hollywood?"

Dan sipped the Amaretto before he answered. "Sorry to disappoint you," he said, "but nothing that socially redeeming." His instincts were sharp, honed by years on the street. He had instantly seen and recognized Brendan's upper-class misgivings and he was not above enjoying the opportunity to puncture some of his misconceptions. "Remember that stream of kung fu movies that came out during the seventies?" Brendan nodded. "I appeared in a few of them and was technical advisor on a hell of a lot more."

"You were in Hollywood?" Brendan was still two beats behind in the conversation.

Stefanie was silent but inside she bubbled with laughter. When it came to Hollywood and the film industry, Brendan was like a small boy at a double feature. Anything and everything to do with the silver screen fascinated him.

"Have you ever met Ali MacGraw?" Brendan asked. Dan nodded. "Linda Evans?" Dan nodded again. Brendan leaned forward. His hazel eyes danced with excitement. "How about Raquel Welch?"

Dan grinned with delight. "Her too," he answered.

Brendan was muttering things like, "Boy, what a life!" and Dan was obviously enjoying the whole thing.

Stefanie tapped him on the shoulder.

"Tom Selleck?" She rolled her eyes and sighed theatrically.

Dan's dark blue eyes zeroed in on her. "Him, too."

"And—?" She feigned breathless anticipation.

"Would you believe me if I told you he was really five feet six inches tall and totally bald?"

She grinned at him. "Would you want me to believe you?"

Brendan had called Paula over and was busy order-
ing another round of Amarettos and more coffee. Dan
lowered his voice so only Stefanie could hear him.

"Yes," he said. "I'd also like you to believe Rob-
ert Redford is gay, Paul Newman wears contact lenses,
and Stallone's body is airbrushed."

"I believe," she said, her voice softer, more yielding. "I believe."

She could sense that it was only Brendan's presence
that kept him from leaning across the table and seal-
ing their wordless declaration with the kiss that had
hovered so long between them. Anticipation, she was
discovering, carried more of an erotic charge than she
would have imagined possible.

"What about Victoria Principal?" Brendan's full
attention was, for the moment, back on Dan. "Is
she—sorry, Red—built as great as she looks?"

They were off and running, and for the next hour
Stefanie found herself as enthralled as her brother was
by Dan's Hollywood stories. He had them laughing
over some of the hassles connected with filming kung
fu scenes in a swimming pool, of performing crazy
vaulting leaps over upended cars, and being expected
to hit the ground ready to fight.

"You have no idea what magic film editors can
perform," he said, shaking his head. "They can turn
mistakes into stunts you would not believe."

Brendan looked disappointed. "You mean a lot of
those flying leaps are impossible?" He looked like
he'd just been told there was no Santa Claus.

"Not impossible," Dan said, "just highly improb-
able in those situations."

"Can you do a flying side kick?" Stefanie asked.

He looked over at her. "I sure can. It gets harder every year, but I can still do it."

"Could you show us?" Brendan asked.

Dan looked around the small restaurant "Here?"

"Not here," Brendan said. "How about the parking lot?"

Stefanie leaned forward, enchanted with the idea of seeing his body in motion once again. "Would you? I know Brendan would love it."

Dan shrugged and motioned Paula over with the check. "Why not? I guess I'm still a ham at heart."

The look Dan gave Stefanie said something else again as they filed out of the restaurant and into the parking lot behind the building. He knew she wanted to see his graceful body in motion, wanted to see him do what he did so well, and he was going to oblige her, but he wanted her to know he understood full well the implication in her request.

Stefanie and Brendan leaned against the trunk of his Porsche. The air was chilly and she shivered, but the shiver had less to do with the temperature than with anticipation. He had stripped off his leather jacket and she held it, her fingers stroking the smooth, silky leather.

He stood still for a moment in the center of a pool of light from the lone streetlamp, then without any preliminaries—indeed, it seemed without any effort at all—his body glided through the air, one knee sharply bent with foot drawn in toward his thigh, the other leg fully extended with balletic grace and precision. He landed a few feet away from them and threw his head back and laughed as they applauded and cheered as they walked over to him.

"Man! That is something else!" Brendan clapped Dan on the back. "You're damn good."

Dan thanked him and scraped his curly hair off his forehead.

"*Sensi* is a master of his art," Stefanie said, her voice huskier than before. The sudden strength and agility he had at his command had rocketed through her body, making her wonder what other marvelous surprises a man like Dan could possess.

He looked down at her, a smile of surprise at the edges of his full mouth. "A compliment from Ms. Colt? You surprise me." The grin turned into a small smile. "Have I made a believer of you?"

Oh, yes, she thought. *I believe you can do anything.* But what she said was: "A man who defies gravity earns my respect."

Brendan looked at his watch. "Listen, it's after eleven. I had a great time, but I'll just make it back to JFK to hitch a ride back to Boston on Dad's plane." He held out his hand and Dan shook it heartily. "I really enjoyed meeting you," he said, and Stefanie was pleased to see her brother meant his words.

"Next time you're here," Dan said, "call me and I'll show you the videotape of the swimming pool scene."

"Will do."

Stefanie stepped forward to kiss her brother good-bye. Dan had moved away and was busying himself rearranging something or other in the trunk of his

Porsche, allowing brother and sister a few moments for personal conversation.

She hugged Brendan and kissed his cheek. "Well?" she whispered in his ear.

"I was wrong. He's a nice guy. But that still doesn't mean he's right for you." He hugged her close. "Take it slow, Red. Examine your motives. He's not like the men you've dated before."

"We're not dating," she said. "There's nothing between us."

The word yet hung unspoken in the air between them.

"There will be," Brendan said. Stefanie blushed but didn't deny it. "Only a fool would think otherwise."

Once again she shivered and wrapped her arms around her body. "You're not a fool," she said, acknowledging the truth of his words, "and neither am I."

Brendan got into his rented car and started the engine. He beeped his horn twice then drove slowly out of the parking lot. After his taillights disappeared, Stefanie turned around and found Dan standing, not twenty feet away by the Porsche, but only steps away from her side.

And from the look on his face, she knew at once that he had heard every word.

9

She stared at him across the few feet that separated them. The lone streetlamp was shining in her eyes and she felt like a wild animal trapped in the headlights of an oncoming car, vulnerable and exposed.

"I wasn't eavesdropping," he said, closing the distance between them. "It's very quiet here and your voices carried."

She was silent. He could see her embarrassment was profound, but she didn't move away as he came closer.

"There will be something between us, won't there, Stefanie?"

His words mingled with the night breeze and caressed her cheek.

"Only a fool would think otherwise," she said softly, repeating her brother's words of a few moments ago.

Her lips were slightly parted and he knew she expected him to kiss her. He also knew that this was neither the time nor the place because once he set his desire in motion, he doubted he'd be able to stop the process.

There was a noise behind them as some of the restaurant's workers, chatting and laughing, headed toward their cars to go home. Paula notice them and waved and Dan waved back. Stefanie watched her start her old Buick, then looked back at Dan.

"We have a new tradition," she said. "Being interrupted."

He drew his index finger across her lips, over her chin, and down her long throat. "When the time is right, there will be no interruptions," he said, lips brushing her earlobe. "I promise you that."

"Two more weeks," she said, touching his hand for one perfect second.

"Thirteen days," he answered. "Then we make our own rules."

If her life had been an old movie, the next thirteen days would have been shown by the pages of a calendar being scattered to a capricious wind. Time slowed and each day—each night—brought her closer to her reckoning. Work kept her busy by day and she took class two nights a week and found perverse pleasure in Dan's nearness, enjoying a fiercely painful sharpening of her senses at being so near him without being near at all.

Watching his body flow from movement to movement as he explained the actions that would form the basis of a self-defense technique, she felt she could actually see the *ki,* or life force, emanating from him. Once he articulated a kung fu movement and she could actually visualize a bird in the lines of his up-raised and curved hand, fingers rounding into the beak.

It was an exquisite form of torture, unlike any other she had ever endured. Surely the rack or pillory were as children's imaginings compared to what pain building desires could produce.

The only thing that eased her pain was the fact that he suffered as much as she did. She could tell by the sharp intake of his breath when her breast brushed against his arm during a hold or by the way his pupils dilated each time the scent of her perfume reached him unexpectedly. She had known power in the business world, but it hadn't prepared her for the heady sensation of wielding sexual and sensual power over a man.

Over Dan.

He was strong, but in this she was the stronger. On a certain unalloyed primitive level the female of the species reigned supreme, and she knew she had the ability to disorient him with a touch, to intoxicate him with a look.

Desire pierced at her and drew blood, and it pleased her to know that he felt the edge of the sword as well.

"I hope it works." Jack Conway, head of Conway's international division, leaned over and frowned at the maze of wires attached to the telephone console system set up in the conference room.

Stefanie ran a hand along her waist band to make sure her ivory silk blouse was tucked neatly into the skirt of her best black pin-striped suit. This was one day where she hoped the clothes would help make the woman, because her concentration was not the best of late.

"We've used teleconferencing many times with great success, Jack," she said as she arranged the stacks of photocopied ledger sheets in piles near her chair. "It's infinitely more cost efficient than making field trips to four different cities."

Conway looked unconvinced as he picked up the agenda sheet from the pile. "I hope you're right," he said. "I'm from the old school of slugging out your differences face to face."

She pointed to the enormous screen at the far end of the room and smiled. "We will be face to face, Jack. This is teleconferencing."

"I'm just not sure," he said.

Once more she realized how near she had come to a showdown with both Tele-Com and Conway.

"If this doesn't work out to your satisfaction," she said in the supersmooth sales voice she saved for special occasions, "you can go back to that system next quarter." She smiled at the man, who still seemed unconvinced. "I think you'll be pleasantly surprised by this, though."

She, in fact, was the one who was surprised she'd been able to pull off the teleconferencing idea at all. Conway was not known for innovative thinking, and she had had to do a fair amount of wheedling, promising, and near-pandering to convince them to give it a try. When Jack Conway had approached her the week before and said he would like her to do a four-city sweep, she had bolted like a skittish pony. For the first time since the assault on her, it hadn't been fear that had governed her decision. Instead it had been the unshakable conviction that nothing, no power beyond that of her own desire, would keep her from being with Dan on the night of her last class.

She had a strong sense of responsibility toward Tele-Com and, as a result, toward Conway News Service, but she was beginning to allow herself the luxury of responsibility toward herself. It was ironic, but her fears had enabled her to take a step back from her business life for the first time in the years since she left MIT's graduate school. She had talent for business— that was undeniable—and, in her family, vocation was destiny. No one save Brendan had ever seriously given voice to the idea that fulfillment could lie in places other than the courtroom or boardroom.

Even if nothing came of their budding relationship, Stefanie owed Dan a debt of gratitude. In giving her the gift of personal safety, he was also giving her the freedom to make a rational decision as to whether or not to remain with Tele-Com. Just a few weeks ago she had been ready to quit her job rather than be forced into that trip to Hawaii in November. Now she was beginning to believe she would be able to make that trip and, once it was done, be free to decide what direction her life would follow.

The conference attendees began filing in and already the room quivered with the smell of tobacco and power. With a sigh Stefanie carefully put her heart away and got back down to business.

* * *

"You're telegraphing, Marie."

Dan walked over to the petite blond woman who was working with Mike on the techniques of disarming an attacker.

"Your movements were too hard, too abrupt." He demonstrated the angular, quick movements she had made. "We want softness," he said, repeating the same gestures in a fluid, calm fashion that was more effective than outright aggression. "Softness can't be defended against," he said, proving his point by doing the technique both ways with the woman and succeeding only with softness. "You can control the situation quietly and easily." He stepped back. "Now, all of you try again."

He couldn't help it. His eyes strayed for the thousandth time to the large round clock that hung over the door to the *dojo*. It was nearly eight o'clock. Stefanie was an hour late. Actually, later than that. In the past weeks she had grown into the habit of arriving early, ostensibly to change from business suit to *gi*, but he had assumed, perhaps unjustifiably, that it was also to be near him for a while before the other students and teachers arrived. God knew, he had grown to anticipate those few minutes alone with her with the same thrill he had once thought reserved only for lovemaking. Just being close enough to smell the perfume she always wore made him ache with desire. Some nights he'd had to call upon all of the self-control techniques he'd ever learned to keep from covering her body with his, from kissing her, making love to her, until she cried out.

But there were rules and he'd said he would obey them.

He had never been like this with a woman before, but then, there had never been a Stefanie Colt in his life before. A large part of him was still the tough kid from the North End of Boston and for a woman like her to appreciate the man he'd become—it was more than he'd ever imagined possible in his lifetime.

He glanced again at the clock. Five after. *Calm down,* he cautioned himself. *She'll be here.*

Class was over.

The last student was heading toward the front door and Mike was straightening up the *dojo* so it would be ready for tomorrow morning's classes. Dan was sprawled on the couch in his tiny office, head thrown back against the armrest. There was a tap on his office door.

"Everything's all done," Mike said, popping his head in the door. "Should I lock up?"

Dan shook his head. "No, that's okay. I'll do it when I go."

"Tough session, wasn't it?" Mike was used to the pressures a last class usually provided Dan.

"You got it," Dan answered, still reclining on the black sofa. "I'm going to hit the showers then hit the sack. See you tomorrow."

Mike said good night and Dan listened as his footsteps faded down the hallway and the outer door slammed shut behind him.

Dan took his obligations to his students seriously, and it had taken an enormous amount of mental control to push his worries over Stefanie aside and give the students his full attention. The last class was his chance to meld philosophies of personal safety with the physical application of these techniques. It was the class where he had to instill the awareness that learning to avoid danger was ultimately more important than knowing how to fight your way out of danger.

He couldn't relax. She hadn't called. She would have called if she were able to. Something awful had happened. He could feel it snaking its way through his body like a rapacious disease. He hadn't done his job right, hadn't been what he could have been, what he should have been for her.

The front door chimed as someone opened it.

He got up. "Forget something, Mike?"

He opened the door to his office and looked down the length of the hallway. She stood there, balancing her briefcase and gym bag and purse while she tried to close her dripping umbrella, and he felt himself drowning in relief that she was safe, that she was there.

Yet all he could manage were two clipped words: "It's you."

The smile that had illuminated her face when she first saw him flickered a moment, then went out. Uncertainty replaced it but he couldn't allow himself to respond. Violent emotions flamed through him and he didn't trust himself.

"I'm so sorry, Dan," she began, managing to get the wet umbrella closed. "We had a teleconference this afternoon and I couldn't break away and then I got tapped to take one of the sales reps from Cincinnati out to MacArthur Airport—" She shrugged prettily. "Well, you know."

"You could have called."

She smiled again, shyer this time. "I would have, Dan, but I know you hate to be interrupted during class to answer the phone."

He turned away so he could bury his emotions in righteous indignation. "Go change," he said. "You have a class to make up."

"As you wish, *Sensei*." Her voice was clipped and cool as the October night. Damn him. What was the matter with him, anyway?

She stormed into the dressing room and began pulling off her skirt, stripping off her blouse, and replacing them with the loose, sexless karate costume. As she had noticed on Dan the first night she met him, the top of the *gi* had a tendency to fall open and she had made a habit of wearing a close-fitting T-shirt underneath it. However, in her haste to get to work this morning she'd forgotten to take it out of the clothes dryer and toss it in her gym bag. She looked down at the oversized wraparound top; the low V of the neckline exposed the lacy top of her bra and she had to tug and pull it in order to rearrange the top in a way that covered her.

As she pulled her hair back into an unobtrusive braid, she became aware of the intensity of the silence in the studio. The only sound she could make out was the thud of the punching bag in the *dojo* as Dan practiced his kicks.

So this was it, she thought as she made her way down the hallway like a foot soldier on his way to his last battle. All the waiting, all the delicious hours of anticipation—all gone up in smoke.

Just let me get through this without crying.

* * *

He was zeroing in on a spot past the bag, focusing all of his energies on it, and his kicks came straight and hard and true. His training allowed him to recover the concentration needed when he heard the creak from the swinging doors, but, nevertheless, he was still acutely aware of her presence as she entered the room. She carried with her an aura of intensity that seemed to penetrate into his brain, make him want to do better, be better, be more valuable in her eyes.

He turned around to face her. She looked uncomfortable as her arms went to encircle her body then fluttered uselessly, her hands playing with the sash of her *gi*. He wanted to enfold her in his embrace, tell her about all the crazy imaginings he'd been tortured with that evening, but he couldn't form the words. He'd felt pain and loneliness before, but he suddenly knew that without her he would be more lost than he'd ever imagined possible.

He drew a deep breath.

"Hands at your side."

She looked at him, eyes wide. "You don't have to do this, *Sensei*. You must be tired after class. I can—"

His face was impassive. "You signed up for six classes. This—" he gestured broadly "—is your sixth class. Now, hands at side. Ten blocks, alternate left and right, ten palm strikes in double combination. Begin."

He did them with her, his blows fast and sharp. She knew now she couldn't match his speed or style, but, through his encouragement and training, she had found a method that was efficient and effective for her. She finished the exercise with a flourish, feeling her adrenaline flowing through her tired body.

From the utility closet he pulled out the padded vinyl board and slipped it over his forearm. She held her hands palm up at waist level and bent her knees slightly, waiting for instruction. His dark blue eyes locked with hers and she felt anger begin to flow along with the adrenaline. She'd give him as good as she got.

"Center yourself." His voice pierced her concentration. "Give me combinations. Now."

Two rights.

"Is that a slap or a punch?"

"It's a punch." Her voice betrayed her anger. She threw another one, but it was off-center, deflecting upward.

"Where's the follow-through? Visualize a point beyond the board and go for it."

His head was directly behind the board. She visualized it. She set herself, then delivered a sharp blow that cracked against the board.

"Visualization is a marvelous tool," she said calmly. "You have no idea how much it helped me."

She followed up her words with another stinging series of strikes that left him shaking his head in bemusement.

"You've got it," he said, removing the board and shaking out his arm. "Remind me to ask you how you learned to visualize so well."

She looked at him and leveled him with her green eyes. "No big secret," she said. "Your head was right in the line of fire."

For one of the longest moments she'd ever known, he stared at her. *I've gone too far,* she thought. He deserved it, but Stefanie hadn't wanted her fantasy to end on such a sour note.

But then just as she felt herself on the verge of tears, he began to laugh, great whoops of laughter, that carried both the essence of happiness and the fear that came before it.

"I deserved that, didn't I?" he asked when he could speak again.

She nodded and wiped tears of laughter from her own eyes. "Probably years overdue," she said wryly. "I can imagine a line of students signing up for the privilege of knocking *Sensei*'s block off."

He yanked off his sweatband, dangling it between his fingers. "I was that bad tonight?"

"Worse."

"You should have called."

"I can see that now. I'm sorry." She smiled up at him. "You were worried about me, weren't you?"

He looked away for a moment. "Well, after a while I was a little afraid something might have happened."

She struck a defensive posture he had taught her. "To me?" she asked with mock concern. "I can whip my weight in Ninja warriors."

"I know you can, Stefanie," he said with a smile. "After all, who was your teacher?"

She threw two imaginary punches. "Then what on earth were you afraid of?" Her voice still held a teasing edge.

"That you had changed your mind."

"How could I have changed my mind?" she asked. "I've heard this last class is very important for a student."

"It is," he agreed, moving closer to her. "We covered some very important concepts tonight."

A fluttering, not at all unpleasant, began in the pit of her stomach. "Such as?"

"Softness," he said, his voice unsuccessful in hiding the wild surge of desire inside him. "How a man can't defend himself against softness."

She tried to take a deep breath to compose herself, but he was too near and she was too filled with emotion. He ran his hand just over the swell of her breasts, barely covered by the top of her *gi*.

"This is softness," he said.

She slipped her hands inside the top of his black outfit and spread her fingers over the muscles she had fantasized about for so long. His heart pounded beneath her palm.

"And this," she said, pressing her fingers more strongly against him, "is not."

He pulled her to him until her breasts pillowed out against his chest. "I feel like I've waited all my life to hold you."

His words startled both of them with their intensity.

"*Coup de foudre,*" she said.

"What?" His arms held her more tightly.

"The lightning bolt," she explained, fitting her hips against his. "I felt it the second I saw you."

"The past two weeks have been hell." His lips rested near the curve of her ear and the sensation of his breath against the sensitive flesh made her blood flow more quickly.

She touched her lips to the tanned flesh just below the edge of his well-trimmed beard. "And what will our rules be now?"

"To excite," he said, kissing her gently. "To please." *To love.*

He tilted his head slightly and moved toward her. A long sigh of anticipation escaped her lips as she raised her head. The kiss was tentative at first, neither one of them certain of the other's reaction. His beard and mustache brushed against her skin and she chuckled.

"Tickles?"

"No," she said. They hadn't really broken the kiss and their words vibrated against their lips in a way she found almost unbearably erotic. "The opposite—it's soft, so marvelous—"

"And I was ready to shave—"

"Never," she murmured, moving closer still. "It would be criminal."

Tentative was no longer good enough. His hands moved up her spine and every place he touched became a new erogenous zone. She drew one fingernail lightly down his chest, barely touching the nest of curly hairs that matted it, and she delighted in the way he shuddered at her caress. He had moved his mouth a fraction away from hers and his tongue traced the outline of her lips over and over until she felt certain she would spontaneously combust. He maneuvered her a few steps back until her spine rested against the wall near the doorway. He placed a hand on the paneled wall at either side of her head and bent down to look directly into her eyes. He seemed a little wild now, a little dangerous, and she felt a surge of pure lust that made her burn.

"In another moment there will be no stopping or turning back." No part of his body was touching her and desire made her feel half-crazed. "I want you to be sure."

She closed her eyes. "Oh, Dan, I'm sure," she groaned in a voice she'd never heard before. It seemed to reach her from some place beyond herself, some untapped, unimagined place. "I want you, Dan."

His mouth closed over hers with all the power of passion long denied. She wrapped her arms around his neck, fingers reveling in the feel of the thick dark curls. She was ablaze with sensation, a slave to the desires he set in motion. His tongue took full possession of her mouth and she molded her lips around it, pulsing, teasing, until she thrilled to the shudder that racked his body.

He leaned into her and she felt fire snap and blaze against her stomach.

"I want to feel you," he said, ripping off the top of his *gi* with one slashing movement. "I want there to be nothing between us."

Years of education and civilization fell off her like the clothing that dropped to the floor at her bare feet. She felt primitive, awed by the throbbing power of desire, by the insensate need that fired through her.

There was no time for them to admire one another's bodies, to appreciate the nuance of shape and form. Touch was most important. She needed to be touched everywhere, to have him touch her in all ways possible.

The paneling was cool against her backbone—the only part of her body that was not aflame. He lifted her breasts in the palms of his hands—those gentle terrifying hands that could caress or crush at will—and lowered his face to bury himself in softness and scent. He nuzzled in deeper and the feel of his beard against her skin made her moan.

"This?" he asked, mouth against the deep and narrow valley between her breasts, as he stroked her with his beard.

"Yes," she managed. "Oh, Dan, I can't think any longer—"

"Don't think." He was moving lower, moving hungrily, devastatingly toward her navel and beyond.

Her mind was exploding. Bits of conversations, pieces of a long-ago song—all her past thoughts were spinning around her, disappearing. He was stripping her of everything, every last vestige of her old realities.

His face was buried against the warm and moist top of her thighs. She clutched at his shoulders for support as her legs began trembling violently. The intensity, the throbbing primitive power of him was going to kill her, would—

"Stop, please—I need to breathe. I can't think with you kissing me like that—"

He insinuated his way up her body, never breaking the tactile connection between them. "Don't breathe," he said, his voice deeper, more commanding than ever.

"Don't think. There's nothing beyond this, only this power we have over each other."

Again he pressed her back against the paneling, cradling her head gently with one hand while his mouth nipped and demanded a response from her that she would never have believed herself capable of. She burned for him; her body was consuming itself with passion.

"Now." That couldn't be her voice, not that near-animal plea for consummation.

"In my office." His voice was almost a growl. "The couch."

Her nails raked his taut buttocks. "Now," she repeated. "Here. I'm burning, Dan . . ."

They went beyond words. They knew no words to convey the elemental desires thundering through them. His hands spanned her hips and he lifted her slightly, then brought her gently lower until they both gasped in wonder. Her head was thrown back, those heavy-lidded green eyes watching him, devouring him, exciting him—

They needed nothing more than the initial act of joining their bodies to bring them both down to the source of the heat. Stefanie shuddered as waves of electricity flowed through her. She sagged against Dan finally and his legs, as shaky as hers, threatened to buckle.

Gently he eased her away from him, straightened up, then scooped her into his arms.

"We need a place to be," he said, heading into the hallway.

She nodded, sensuous aftershocks of their fiery joining keeping her suspended somewhere near Saturn or Venus.

If the world ended at that moment, as he carried her into his office then lay with her on the black couch, she doubted she would even have noticed.

10

Dan hadn't slept. He had lain awake all night, holding Stefanie close in his arms. He should have been tired for he'd been up over twenty-four hours, but instead he found himself suffused with a strange kind of peaceful energy that kept him awake yet content to remain still. Outside the first birds began to sing and soon he knew light would stream through the windows and this night would be over. He wasn't a man given to poetic leaps of expression, but if it were possible to hold the sun suspended below the horizon, he would risk feeling its fire if it meant keeping her in his arms a moment longer.

It had grown chilly during the night and he'd found a clean but faded quilt on the top shelf of a closet and covered them with it. He could see only the top of her red head and her small straight nose with its light sprinkling of freckles, yet the memory of her body burned behind his eyelids.

She had given herself to him without reservation and he knew that, for her, trust was a factor that loomed as large as desire in her decision to be with him. He had known almost at once that it had been a long time since she'd taken a lover—a slight hesitation, a look of vulnerability that he'd found devastating. Her passion matched his, and her desire to please him and be pleased by him was a potent aphrodisiac; but his need for her had not been easily satisfied and it wasn't now. Desire still nipped at the edges of his consciousness. However, as he gently stroked her back beneath the cover, he found erotic sensation replaced by something stronger, more intense. He wanted to protect her, yet he longed to teach her to protect herself. He wanted to make love to the woman who turned him to fire, yet he wanted to hold the young girl who lived inside her heart.

He had originally planned an exquisite seduction, orchestrating mood and setting, candlelight and champagne, but he had long ago learned that when the moment was as right as that moment had been between them, the trappings of romance were ultimately unimportant. She brought with her enough beauty and joy to turn even his stark office into paradise.

She stirred against him. One of her legs nestled between his, her foot resting on his calf. In the past he had started his relationship in bed and gone on from there, moving from woman to woman, searching for something he couldn't define. Since the death of his brother Michael, he had been reluctant to connect too closely with anyone. This time, though, he had learned of the woman, the human being, first, and the lovemaking that followed was beyond anything in his imaginings. She stirred again and he knew she would awaken at any moment. He wanted to be the first thing she saw, the first sensation she experienced that morning. He wanted it to be as wonderful in the daylight as it had been in the darkness. He spoke.

"Good morning."

Dan's voice reached her as if from a great distance. For hours she'd been in a twilight world, suspended in a place of the flesh and all its infinite delights.

She opened her eyes. Yellow ribbons of early sunlight filtered through the shuttered windows across the room and threw striped shadows over his face and chest. Vivid images of how he had looked, how he had sounded as she had grown acquainted with every inch of his body, filled her mind and she shut her eyes again.

"Good morning," she murmured, suddenly embarrassed and awkward.

Her left arm had been pinned beneath her and she stretched a little to release it, remembering the narrowness of the couch and the marvelous ways they had discovered to circumvent that.

"I like the way you do that." His hand swept along her spine and over the curve of her buttocks, cupping her and pulling her closer to him.

She inhaled deeply at his touch. He smelled a little salty, very male. The scent of love lingered in the small office, unmistakable, intoxicating. No cologne on earth could possess the magical properties his natural scent held for her. She was suddenly aware of her nakedness beneath the quilt, of the fact that what she assumed was a common experience for Dan had been a miracle for her.

She sat up, quilt tucked around her, and squinted at her watch, which, incongruously, was all she wore.

"What time is it?" His voice was casual, but she was suddenly convinced she could detect an undercurrent of anxiety in it.

"Six twenty-nine," she answered. The quilt had dropped below her breasts and she quickly pulled it back around her. Last night she had been nude, but in the morning light she felt simply naked.

Where's the self-help book for the morning after? she wondered as she stood up, drawing the cover around her body from shoulders to calves. She found ironic humor in the fact that a manual existed for every problem from anorexia to zoophobia, but nowhere was there a book that told a woman how to will herself into her clothes and make a graceful exit. For the first time in her life she wished she'd led a more casual love life. Maybe then this ending wouldn't hurt so much.

He must be counting the minutes until she left, she thought. She couldn't remember if he'd even asked her to stay the night—maybe she'd just fallen asleep on his couch and he'd been too much of a gentleman to ask her to leave.

She'd make it easy for him.

"Well," she said with a smile as fake as a plastic philodendron, "I'd better get home and shower and change." He didn't say a word, just watched her, his dark blue eyes hooded and wary beneath the thick fringe of lashes. Why wouldn't he make it easy for her? "I have to be at work by eight thirty, so I—" Her voice trailed off as she suddenly became aware of his body.

He lay naked on the couch, for she had taken the cover with her when she stood up. His beautifully

muscled body was in sharp relief against the black
fabric. She couldn't control her eyes as they swept over
his shoulders, across his broad chest, down his belly.
Then they stopped. What had once been throbbing
and powerful now lay gentle against his thigh. Suddenly he wasn't the man of sexual fire of the night before, but someone as vulnerable as she. When she
stripped him of his covering, she had left him exposed to her eyes and he had allowed her to see him
not just when he was in the powerful arms of desire,
but when he was just a man. Her heart turned over.

Oh, God, she thought. *I've fallen in love with him.*

For a long moment she couldn't move. She stood
there in the middle of his office like a statue, the quilt
exposing one arm and one shoulder, Diana with the
bow arm bare. She didn't want to go but no one had
asked her to stay.

She looked down into his eyes.

"Dan." Part question, part plea.

It was all he'd needed to hear. In the fraction of a
second it took her brain to assimilate what was happening, he had crossed the room and enfolded her in
his arms. He lifted her chin with his hand and kissed
her in a way that made her sure.

"I was wondering if I had dreamed last night," she
said when his lips freed hers for a moment.

He nuzzled beneath her heavy auburn hair.

"Dreams don't smell the way you do," he said, his
voice husky.

She slid her arms over his shoulders and down the
smooth marble of his tanned back. "Or feel the way
you do."

The quilt had fallen to her feet and he pressed her softness against him, moving in a way that made her pulses quicken.

"I wish I didn't have to go," she murmured.

"You don't," he said. "Stay with me."

"I can't. I have work, responsibilities—"

He shook his head and grinned. "Remember when I asked you to spend the weekend with me?"

She grinned back at him. "On the ferry?"

He nodded. "You weren't ready then, but the offer still holds. I'd like the chance to fall the rest of the way in love with you."

Dan's words echoed around in her head and in her heart. He had told her the only thing she needed to know.

"Where's the phone?" she asked, not taking her eyes from him. "I have to call work. I think I'll be needing some time off."

He slid his hands over her midriff and under her breasts, their rounded weight resting lightly over his fingers as he moved her backward toward the couch, which was still warm from their bodies.

"It's too early," he said, covering her body with his own as they sank into the soft cushions. "They don't answer at Conway until eight thirty."

"How do you know?" she asked.

"I have it on good authority."

She opened her eyes in pretend surprise. "Are we going back to sleep, then?" she asked innocently.

He lowered his mouth toward hers.

"Maybe later," he said, his mustache and beard soft against her skin. "Maybe much later."

* * *

Maureen O'Connor Flanagan peered out her kitchen window for what seemed like the tenth time in ten minutes.

"Will you sit down, for heaven's sake?"

Her husband's voice echoed in the quiet room.

"Don't sneak up on me like that!" She held one hand over her throat against her hammering pulse.

Jim looked down at his size twelve-and-a-half feet in workboots and pointedly back up at his wife. "Mo, I couldn't sneak up on a deaf man with feet like this." He crossed the kitchen and slipped his arm round his wife.

"Oh, Jimmy, come on. Not now." She wriggled out of his grasp and stole another peek at the silent street in front of their house. "Dan and Stefanie should be here any minute."

Jim took a container of orange juice out of the refrigerator. He started to take a swig straight from the container, but his wife's murderous glance encouraged him to take a glass down from the cabinet instead.

"Sorry," he said with a slight shrug of his shoulders. "Old Navy habits never die."

"Well, they should," she snapped back at him. "You've been out for thirteen years and you can't remember how to tie a square knot, but you manage to remember every disgusting habit you ever picked up."

He affectionately tugged one of her dark curls but instead of kissing him the way she usually would, she remained distant.

"What's wrong, Mo?" he asked as she paced the kitchen, walking around and around the butcher block worktable in the center. "Dan's just coming by for the keys to his place. That's all."

Maureen turned and looked at him, an odd smile tilting the corners of her mouth.

"He's bringing someone with him. Her name is Stefanie."

Jim shrugged. "He's not a monk, Mo. You've hardly thought he was celibate all these years."

She flushed a little. "You don't understand. I'm sure he's had women in his apartment in New York, but I know he's never brought anyone out to the Cape. That's his home."

Jim extended his hand and his wife placed hers in his. He could feel the tension racing through her.

"Don't go getting your hopes up," he said, drawing her closer. "He may not be the type to settle down." He shook his head as he thought about the man he'd known since their first week in basic training over seventeen years ago. "He hasn't exactly seemed the marrying kind, has he?"

"That's why I know this is different," she said, her voice filled with sisterly conviction. "He doesn't have to come here for the keys. He keeps one hidden beneath the old rowboat in the shed. His subconscious blocked out that fact so he'd have an excuse to bring her here."

Jim laughed. "Mo, cut the amateur shrink act."

"A little pop psychology never hurt anyone," she said and rested her head on her husband's shoulder for a second. "I've known something was happening since Labor Day weekend. We're the only family he has and he wants us to meet her."

Jim remained skeptical although he could see the logic in her argument. "Don't be disappointed if you're wrong, Mo. Please."

She kissed his cheek.

"I won't be," she said looking back out the window for Dan's red Porsche.

Of course I won't be, she thought, *because I won't be wrong at all.*

"I didn't know we were getting the keys from your sister," Stefanie said as she tried to balance a makeup mirror on her knee and refresh her eye shadow in a moving sports car. The car bounced through a large pothole and her mascara and lipstick slipped to the floor. "Don't they ever fix the roads in Rhode Island?"

Dan chuckled. "Don't be so hard on them," he said. "It's a small state. How much income do you think it has to tax?"

She shot him a pointed glance. "You must be kidding! The average family income in Newport would be enough to maintain an emerging nation."

His shoulders shook with laughter and she thought the Porsche would swerve out of its lane.

"It wasn't that funny," she said, adding another coat of peach lipstick.

He looked at her and laughed again. "You're right. It wasn't your sense of humor that got to me. I was thinking of what Maureen and Jim would say if they heard you."

"They live in Newport?"

He nodded.

"How big a house?"

"Nothing spectacular. Five bedrooms, three baths."

"Live-in help?"

"No." He thought for a second. "But someone comes in three times a week to clean."

"A lot of property?"

"I'm no good with numbers. Maybe an acre?"

She scratched her head. "That's a small house. What do they do for a living?"

"Jim is president of a brokerage firm, part of his dad's conglomerate. Maureen used to be an emergency room nurse but she quit last year to try to start a family."

They obviously were moneyed, but the pieces just didn't fit. "There's something missing," she said. "If you live in Newport, you either have a mansion or a yacht or both."

He hesitated. "Well, they do spend a lot of time on their boat—" he began.

"What kind?"

"Forty-seven-foot sloop."

She shot him a satisfied grin. "What did I tell you? Typical Newport."

He swung onto the exit ramp and headed toward the Flanagans' house.

"Are you sure you're not a lawyer?" he asked. "I had the feeling I was getting the third degree."

"I'm not," she said, "but my mother's a lawyer. And my brother Walker, and my brother Harrison, and my brother Brendan—"

He laughed. "What about your father?"

"His business keeps them in business."

"How did you escape the family trade?"

She was silent for a moment before she spoke. "I wasn't very verbal as a child," she said. "Numbers and science appealed more to me. So they programmed me into computer engineering."

He turned down a side street shaded with trees that were starting to turn the vivid reds and yellows of autumn.

"You had no say in the matter?"

"Very little. Brendan was always the rebel in the family; I was the appeaser."

"You seem pretty feisty to me. I can't imagine anyone telling you what to do."

"Family conditioning can be an insidious thing," she said. "Whenever I speak to my mother, I turn into a gawky fourteen-year-old looking for approval. It's only lately that I've begun to realize I have the right to make my own decisions and my own mistakes."

"That's one thing I was good at," he said. "Making mistakes."

She glanced around the inside of the expensive car. "Seems you've done well despite them."

He thought about the people lost each year to the streets, thought about his brother.

"Not well enough," he said. "There've been a few notable failures."

She started to point out how remarkable his success was, especially in view of his lack of formal education, but there was something in his face, an indefinable hint of sadness, that stilled her tongue. How little she knew of him. How much she wanted to learn.

"Two more blocks," he said, making a right onto a street even prettier than the one before. "Last chance to fix your makeup."

She respected his need for privacy and let it pass. Besides, her ulcer had begun to twitch alarmingly as they got closer to his sister's house.

He made another right, then turned into a circular driveway about one hundred feet down the road. A two-story white Colonial beauty with black shutters and flower boxes at every window sat on top of a slight rise of green lawn. It was the kind of house she'd always loved.

He shut the engine off, got out, and hurried around to help her from the low-slung car.

"Dan!" The front door of the house swung open and a woman with hair as dark and curly as Dan's came down the flagstone path toward them. She was tall and long-limbed with an easy physical grace that Stefanie envied immediately.

"They're here, Jimmy!" she called over her shoulder.

She embraced Dan, placing an enormous lipsticked kiss on his cheek.

"You look thin," she said, rubbing the red mark from his cheek with two long fingers. "Are you eating well?"

"Three squares a day plus," he said, catching Stefanie's eyes over his sister's head. "Face up to it, Mo— I'm meant to be lean and mean."

"Mean, I'll agree with," she answered, "but this lean, I don't know."

She turned and Stefanie felt herself being instantly sized up by a pair of warm dark brown eyes.

"I'm Maureen." She extended her hand. "You must be Stefanie."

"I am." She shook the woman's hand. "I'm happy to meet you."

Maureen's eyes strayed for a split second as she watched her husband lope down the long driveway.

"Call me Mo," she said, turning back to Stefanie. "Everyone does."

"Hey, Dan. Good to see you." Jim clapped his brother-in-law on the back.

"Jimmy, this is Stefanie. Dan's friend." Maureen shot her brother a look Stefanie had used many times before on Brendan. "You should have introduced Stefanie to us, Dan."

Dan rolled his eyes heavenward, then looked at Stefanie. "Sisters can be a pain. Have I had a chance to open my mouth since the Bionic Talker came outside?"

"You're not pulling me into this!" Stefanie held her hands palms up and laughed. "I have three brothers myself. I can't violate the unwritten code of sisterhood."

Maureen linked her arm through Stefanie's. "I like you," she said bluntly. "You have spunk."

"Mo's highest accolade," Jim said with a grin. "Heretofore only awarded to Katharine Hepburn and Golda Meir."

Stefanie laughed. "Such exalted company!"

Dan motioned for attention.

"Listen, you guys, I love you both, but we didn't come here to shoot the breeze." He waggled his fingers in front of Maureen's nose. "The keys?"

Maureen dismissed him with an impatient gesture. "Stefanie and I are going to get to know one another while I put up the coffee."

"Mo, they said they wanted the keys."

She gave her husband her best wifely smile. "Why don't you show Danny how the work on the MGB is coming along?"

Dan's eyes suddenly widened. "You started restoring the MGB?"

"You bet." Jim's voice grew animated. The men were quickly forgetting the purpose of Dan's visit. "Al Donato at TPC Auto Parts told me about this new compounding formula that..."

They rounded the corner and Stefanie couldn't make out Jim's words any longer, but she did see the look of resigned humor on Dan's face as he smiled at her before disappearing.

"I apologize for being so heavy-handed," Maureen said as she led the way up the walk and into the side door to the kitchen. "It was the only way I could get to chat with you before Dan whisks you off to the Cape."

Stefanie didn't know what to say to that and was grateful when she entered the lovely country kitchen and found something safe to talk about.

"This is it!" she exclaimed, drawing her hands together and turning around. "The kitchen of my dreams."

Maureen pulled a coffee filter out of a utility drawer. "Mine, too," she said. "I know it's old-fashioned and almost laughable these days to say this, but I've always felt you can hear the heartbeat of a family in its kitchen."

Stefanie looked at the lanky woman in front of her and felt a rush of affection. She tilted her head to the right and listened. "I hear it," she said. "Strong and steady."

"That's us." Maureen measured in a generous amount of special-blend coffee and began to boil the water. "There's a whole untapped field of research a sociologist could look into—reading a family's condition by their pots and pans and dishes."

Stefanie glanced around at the copper pots hanging from the ceiling, the utensils on a wrought-iron rack on the wall, the marigolds all yellow and orange on the windowsill, then thought about her parents' kitchen, which looked like an operating room on "General Hospital."

"I envy you. You seem to have a wonderful life here."

Maureen nodded. A thick shiny curl bobbed over her forehead and she raked it back with a gesture so like her brother's it nearly took Stefanie's breath away.

"I am lucky," she said simply. "Now if we are blessed with children . . ."

Maureen bustled around, pouring hot water into the coffeepot, removing the used filter, taking down two china mugs and placing them on the table. Finally she poured the steaming coffee into them and handed one to Stefanie, who nodded her thanks.

"Dan said you quit work to start a family."

Maureen nodded as she swallowed a sip of coffee. "Fourteen months ago," she said. "My doctor told me that it gets harder to conceive when you're thirty-five. I thought all I had to do was say farewell to my diaphragm and *voilà!* It hasn't been that easy." At the look of embarrassed concern on Stefanie's face, Maureen patted her hand. "Don't worry. We had all the tests and we're both okay. In fact—'' she lowered her voice conspiratorially ''—I think we may just have hit the jackpot this month.''

Stefanie's eyes widened. ''You think you're pregnant?''

Maureen nodded. ''Don't speak so loud! I don't want the Fates to hear us, but Jimmy and I are pretty sure this time we did it.''

''You're so lucky,'' Stefanie said. ''What a marvelous experience to share with the man you love.''

Maureen caught the wistful tone in Stefanie's voice. ''You really mean that, don't you?''

She nodded. ''Does that surprise you?''

''A little. From what Dan told me about you on the phone, I thought you were the high-powered career type.''

Stefanie met the other woman's glance head-on. ''That's my job description, Mo, not who I am.''

Maureen grinned. ''*Touché.*''

Stefanie took another sip of coffee. ''I think Dan said you were an emergency room nurse before you quit.'' Maureen nodded. ''Do you miss it?''

The dark-haired woman thought a moment before she answered. ''Sometimes,'' she said. ''But I had done that—and done it well—for twelve years. When we decided we were ready to have a family, I quit. Don't get me wrong,'' she continued, ''I'm not against working mothers.'' She looked around at the beautiful kitchen with love and Stefanie could feel her words before Maureen gave them voice. ''My mom had to work cleaning houses and we all turned out pretty well. It's just Jim and I are lucky enough to be able to afford the luxury of a full-time mommy and I've waited a long time for this. I want to enjoy every single second I can with him—or her.'' She grinned. ''End of speech.''

''It was a beautiful speech,'' Stefanie said slowly. ''In fact, I could have written it for you. The only difference is my mother didn't have to work but chose to.''

''I thought so. My Irish intuition is pretty good at picking up people's vibes, and I knew I'd found a kindred spirit.''

''A sister iconoclast,'' Stefanie said, laughing.

''This is one of the best things the women's movement did for us,'' Maureen continued. ''Freed us to make real choices. Remember back when women were going to have careers and no children?''

''Right. Then it was career and children simultaneously, no matter who suffered.''

Maureen's dark eyes danced with understanding and humor. ''The Superwoman complex. Then there's the New Wave—us—who think sequentially. I want a career, children, and then more career.''

''That's it,'' Stefanie said. ''If you can afford it, I'm in favor of full-time mothering the first five years. You can keep your hand in your career while the kids are tiny, then phase it all back in later.'' She finished her coffee. ''Mother was back in her office ten days after my brother Brendan and I were born. To this day I hardly know the woman.''

''Do you think that had to do with her career?'' Maureen asked, obviously framing her words with great care. ''Not every woman is cut out for mothering.''

"You're a perceptive lady, Mo. I'm afraid Mother and I are like fire and ice. Always have been, always will be." She grew quiet.

Maureen got up from the table, poured them refills of coffee, then took a platter of roast beef sandwiches out of the refrigerator.

"Danny and our mother went through a spell like that," she said, leaning against the counter. "Our dad died when Dan was in his early teens and he really went off the deep end for a while after it." She shook her head, remembering. "It wasn't until he was arrested for petty larceny and our brother Michael stepped in and became a surrogate father that it began to—"

She was interrupted by Dan and Jim, who burst through the kitchen door laughing.

"Hand those keys over, Mo. It's time for Ms. Colt and I to hit the road."

"You can stay for something to eat, can't you?" Maureen asked as she took oval sandwich platters from the cupboard.

Dan grabbed a sandwich half for himself then handed one to Stefanie.

"Two sandwiches to go, Mrs. Flanagan. Now, where are the keys?"

Maureen looked over at Jim for support.

"Can you convince them to stay?"

"I'm not even going to try, Mo." He drew his wife toward him and ruffled her dark curls. "They want to be alone, dopey."

Maureen, who had been honestly enchanted by getting to know Stefanie, buried her face against Jim's face and groaned. "I've been married too long," she muttered, loud enough for everyone to hear. "The keys are hanging on the pegboard." She looked at Dan. "Forgive me?"

He chucked her under the chin. "Always."

Jim flipped him the keys and the four of them trooped down the driveway to the Porsche, men in the lead.

"I didn't mean to delay your weekend," Maureen said as she and Stefanie picked their way through the lawn, which was speckled with fallen leaves. "Believe me, there were no family high jinks going on."

Impulsively Stefanie put her arm around Maureen and hugged her. "I believe you. Besides, I really enjoyed our visit. I don't have many women friends and it was marvelous to share a little girl talk."

They laughed at the old-fashioned term. Dan and Jim were leaning against the side of the red sports car. Afternoon sunlight filtered through the trees and sparkled in Dan's dark hair, which seemed even darker against his brother-in-law's blond good looks. For a second the thought that these people might be part of the rest of her life flickered across her mind, but the thought was too exquisite—and the possibility of it not happening too painful—for her to allow it to linger.

Maureen stopped about twenty feet away from the car and turned to her.

"I think you'll be good for Danny," she said. "Since Michael—well, we've all known he needed a ballast. We've worried about him."

"What do you mean since Michael?"

Maureen glanced away and Stefanie could see the woman had assumed Stefanie had knowledge she didn't possess.

"Listen, I'm sorry. I thought you knew."

Stefanie touched her arm. "Knew what? If it's that important to Dan, I'd like to know."

Dan was on his way to collect Stefanie.

"He was our brother." Maureen's voice was low and rushed and Stefanie hadn't caught the use of the past tense.

"You said that earlier. Where is he? Does he live around here?"

Dan was nearly on top of them.

"He's dead, Stefanie."

There was no time to pursue the topic because Dan was next to her, then suddenly sweeping her into his arms.

"If this is the only way I can get you out of here, so be it."

Maureen's jaw dropped open and Stefanie giggled helplessly as Dan carried her toward his car.

"Put me down, Dan. I'll come peaceably," she said, laughing at the undignified, un-Coltlike sight she made.

"Sorry," he said, carrying her to the Porsche where Jim had the passenger door open and waiting. "I'm not taking any chances." He bent down and plopped her on the seat, then closed the door behind her. He went around to the other side and slid behind the steering wheel. Maureen and Jim, arms around each other, leaned into Stefanie's open window.

"If *Sensei* O'Connor will allow it, why don't you two plan on coming up for dinner a week from Sunday?"

Stefanie looked at Dan, who shrugged with mock resignation.

"Do you think you can stand Mo's pot roast?" he asked.

Stefanie grinned. "Try and keep me away," she said. Maureen kissed her on the cheek and Jim shook her hand. Dan started the engine and the roar of the Porsche nearly drowned out her next words. "I hope you find out you won the jackpot."

Dan looked at her as he threw the car into gear. "What jackpot?"

She looked at Maureen and winked. "I'll tell you later, *Sensei*."

Maureen and Jim backed away from the car and watched as it rolled down the curving driveway, then shot off down the road back toward the highway.

Jim looked at her, his clear blue eyes slightly bemused. "She's the one, isn't she?" he asked, a touch of awe in his voice. "You were right, weren't you?"

"You bet." She leaned against his chest, her hand lightly stroking at her not-yet-rounded belly. Very softly she said, "I think you've just met your future aunt."

11

"**W**ell?" Dan stood in the middle of the living room of his home and watched as Stefanie's green eyes scanned the room.

"I'm flabbergasted," she said. Instead of the starkly modern bachelor's delight she had envisioned, Dan's home on the Cape was just that: a home. She stood in the center of the living room on a braided rug and stared in amazement at the heavy knotty pine paneling that ran from floor to ceiling, at the enormous brick fireplace on the wall to her left, and the overstuffed furniture and bookshelves on the opposite wall.

A tiny muscle in the corner of his jaw twitched. "Is that good or bad?"

She smiled. "Very good. It's just not what I expected."

He relaxed and grinned, tossing his car keys down on the pine coffee table before the Early American sofa. "You expected fur rugs and disco lights?"

She moved toward the enormous bay window that overlooked the windswept dunes and the Atlantic

Ocean at the bottom of the cliff. When they had made the turn onto Pilgrim Road she had gasped at the way the homes seemed suspended on the edge of the cliff, as if they were taunting nature to reclaim her own. She turned back to Dan.

"Of course I expected fur rugs and disco lights," she answered. "Not to mention quadraphonic stereo and a mirrored ceiling."

"You haven't seen the bedroom yet."

Stefanie's eyes widened in alarm.

"You're kidding me, aren't you, Dan?"

"Relax," he said, stepping behind her and wrapping her in an embrace. "I have that in my apartment on the Island. Not here."

She turned her head slightly and looked up and back at him. "I don't want to hear it."

He chuckled. "Come on, Stefanie. I'll tell you all about my sunken tub and water bed."

Her body stiffened in his arms.

"Spare me the details, please."

He released her from his arms. "I was planning on giving you the guided tour when we get back home." She wouldn't look at him. "You know how we poor kids are when we get a little money—go straight for the showiest things in town."

She crossed her arms over her breasts. "I'm not joking, Dan."

His dark brows slid into a scowl. Every now and then he became acutely conscious of the differences in style between them and it alternately frightened and annoyed him. He had meant his statement as a joke but somehow it had not turned out that way. "Where's your sense of humor, kiddo? You can't blame me—I was still under the influence of Tinsel Town when I decorated it." He pried one of her hands free and held on to it. "Don't put up walls between us, Stefanie. There are enough there that we had nothing to do with. Tell me what's wrong."

"I can't stand the thought of you with another woman. Your apartment was obviously not a cloister."

"No, it wasn't."

Her head lifted at the use of the past tense.

"I haven't been with another woman since the day we met."

She felt buoyant with pleasure that she tried to hide. "I would never have dreamed of asking you about that, Dan."

"I know you wouldn't, you stubborn redhead. I wanted you to know." His dark blue eyes seemed to glow from within. "I felt I owed it to you."

She inclined her head in his direction. "Thank you. There's been no one for me either." Her own eyes twinkled. "It needed to be said."

Sometimes she was so formal, so proper in her speech and her ways that it made him feel gauche and foolish. Other times, like now, the same dignified manner moved him almost to tears.

"Were you ever in love, Stefanie?"

"I cared about a man years ago," she said with customary honesty. "But that's long past."

His face seemed to close up. "What happened?"

"We were very young and there were a lot of family considerations involved."

"Your parents broke you up?"

She hesitated. "It's been years, Dan. I was just a girl then."

"And since you've been a woman?"

"No one important. No man has ever come close to what you mean to me."

He stepped close to her and plunged his hands into her thick auburn hair, caressing her scalp.

Funny tugging sensations began in the center of her body as she leaned against him, her hips nestling just below his.

"Nice place you've got here," she murmured, her lips finding a warm spot in the base of his throat.

"Care to see my etchings?" he murmured as his large hands caressed either side of her face, turning it up for his kiss.

Stefanie ran her tongue lightly along the outline of his mouth, which seemed all the more sensual for his beard and mustache. "Is that a proposition, sir?"

"No," he said. "It's gone too far for that. It's a promise."

"We're out of wine." Stefanie tilted the empty bottle of Beaujolais over Dan's bare stomach and watched as two red drops fell onto his tan skin. She had been feeling so well that she was even able to have an occasional glass of wine.

It was sunset on Saturday. Except for occasional forays into other parts of the house for certain unavoidable necessities, they had spent the last twenty-four hours in each other's arms.

"We're out of cheese, too." His voice was lazy, amused.

She bent over him, her auburn hair brushing against his chest, and licked the wine from his body. "Guess we'll have to get dressed and go to the all-night deli."

"Like hell we will." He grabbed her by the shoulders and rolled her over onto her back. "We still have four cans of Pepsi, three eggs, tomato soup, and crackers."

His hands moved over her breasts and she sighed.

"Have you been taking inventory?"

"Of course." His mouth was pressed against the underside of one breast. He looked up at her. "I wanted to know exactly how long I could keep you in my bed without having you die from hunger."

"How little you know, *Sensei*," she said, sliding her hands up his back until they reached his thick curly hair. "It's pleasure I'll die from. You're killing me with pleasure."

He stroked her inner thighs and beyond with a touch so light as to be almost imaginary. She held back a moan of delight. Her body was like finely turned radar, exquisitely sensitive to every whisper of sensation.

"Tell me, Stefanie." His voice was smoky and dark as his eyes. "Tell me what you like."

"When you touch me like that," she said, trailing her index finger down over his cheekbones and to his lips. "I like it when you touch me like that."

"And this?" He straddled her, teasing her by denying her the fullest satisfaction.

She nodded, head thrown back against the white linen pillow. "Yes," she whispered.

She felt him pushing against her and she yearned toward him. Her entire body ached to feel herself close around him, enfolding him.

"What do you want, Stefanie?" He was sitting astride her, most of his weight on his knees so his hands were free to caress her.

"You. I want you."

His burning eyes fanned the flames that seared her limbs. She had lost track of time and place; there was for her no reality beyond this small house on a cliff overlooking the ocean, beyond this wide soft bed on which they lay together. She felt the old Stefanie slipping away, farther and farther out of reach, while a newer, more sensual woman took her place.

She focused directly on his face, that face that had suddenly become the center of a swirling universe, and arched her hips slightly to meet him.

"I want to feel you inside me, Dan," she said, her voice soft but sure. "I want there to be nothing between us. I want you to blot out everything else in the world but us."

He grasped her hips in his hands and pulled her body closer to him until he was deep inside her. She didn't close her eyes; instead she watched as he moved slowly, the muscles in his chest and abdomen moving beneath his skin with every motion. Her body recognized something that she herself had not yet come to admit. She had found her mate. The feeling inside her was primeval; it went beyond language and culture and the civilized trappings of modern life. On the most elemental level she understood why an animal would kill in defense of her mate. She ached to possess all of him, to be able to enfold him body and soul, a strange blending of maternal and sexual passions that stirred her soul. He satisfied every part of her.

But his hunger for her wasn't as easily satisfied. After he had driven her halfway to madness, reducing her to pliant sensuality, he withdrew from her and lay down on the bed, pulling her on top of him until her breasts grazed the mat of curls on his chest. She thought she would faint from the undischarged electricity coursing through her. He tried to move her hips on top of his but she moved slightly out of reach and drew her hand down his belly, watching him quiver beneath her fingers.

He murmured an endearment she didn't understand and urged her to straddle him once again. Instead she slid down the length of his body, her breasts sliding across his stomach, his thighs, his knees, until she knelt between the juncture of his legs. He raised himself up on one elbow to see her face. She brushed her hair off her forehead and smiled, her tongue flicking at the corner of her kiss-swollen mouth.

Slowly her hands stroked him, long voluptuous movements that made the muscles of his thighs tighten as she swept under then over the most sensitive of areas. His arm was thrown across his face as if to shield his eyes from the face of the sun. She leaned forward and her hair fell across his belly as she lowered her mouth to him. Her lips touched his warm skin and she could feel the rapid pulsing of his blood. His smell was musky with the blend of their mingled desires. She closed her eyes, and vivid reds and yellows flamed against her lids. He trembled beneath her and his moans grew louder as her hands and mouth worked magic, wove dreams, conjured visions of other dimensions of pleasure.

She was all-powerful. She delighted in the fact that she could take this man and make him quiver beneath her the way she had willingly trembled for him. Excitement blinded her. Passion roared in her ears like the ocean crashing into the rocks below their window.

All she knew was she would pleasure him in all ways.

Always.

"Michael."

At the sound of Dan's voice next to her she was instantly awake, but she had trouble placing herself in time and space. For the first time in years she had let herself flow freely through the hours and, without her wristwatch, she had lost all perception of time. He moaned slightly.

"Dan?" She gently touched his shoulder. "Are you all right?"

He didn't respond, just moved restlessly next to her. She leaned over to look at him. The room was bathed in the eerie grays and blues of the predawn hours and outside a fierce wind whistled up the dunes and rattled the window frames of the small house. He groaned again and flipped over onto his back. His curly hair flopped across his forehead and some of the strands were dark with sweat. She lay back down next to him, curling her body along the straight line of his hip.

"Michael," he said again. "Michael!"

Dan's body began to tremble, not much at first, just a subtle shiver. She placed her hand on his chest; his flesh seemed cool yet there was a sheen of sweat. She could see the rapid eye movements behind his closed lids and she knew he was deep inside the private world of dreams. His hands were clenched in fists at his sides. She hesitated, wanting to release him from his nightmare but uncertain. Before she had a chance to act, he emitted a low howl of pain unlike anything she'd ever heard, then sat bolt upright, his eyes staring into a hell she knew nothing about.

"Oh, Dan—sweetheart, what is it?" The endearment, unusual for her, had sprung to her lips naturally.

He looked at her without recognition and she read terror and sorrow in his eyes. It took him a full ten seconds before she felt him relax.

"Are you all right?"

He cleared his throat. "Did I say anything?"

She drew closer to him, wrapping one slim arm around his shoulders. "You said a name."

His eyes closed as if even the effort of holding them open was more than he could manage.

"Do you know what name?" she asked.

He nodded and dragged his hand through his tousled hair. The trembling still vibrated against her and she longed to hold him, to ease his sorrows the way he had erased her fears.

I can help you, she whispered silently. *Let me inside your heart.*

He threw the covers aside and swung his feet to the floor.

"Don't go, Dan."

"I'm awake," he said. "I'm going to have some coffee."

"Fine." She swung her own feet to the floor and reached for her nightgown, which was tossed over the back of the rocking chair that faced the fireplace. "I could use a cup, too." She walked around to his side of the bed and held out her hand. "Coming?"

He looked at her but didn't take her hand. A chill blossomed inside her chest.

"Go back to sleep," he said. "It's not even sunrise yet."

She carefully sat down next to him as if by not disturbing the bedcovers she wouldn't be noticed.

"I don't want to go back to sleep, Dan."

He shook his head. "Look," he said, his eyes not quite meeting hers, "I think I'd rather be alone for a while, okay?"

She moved a fraction closer to him, her heart aching. She rested her head against the smooth skin of his shoulder. "I've grown accustomed to feeling you next to me this weekend, Dan. We only have a few more hours before we return to the real world."

He inhaled, a deep shuddering breath, then managed a smile. "Are you telling me I'm nothing more than a three-night stand, lady?"

She curled across his lap, the silky folds of her nightgown falling across his legs and knees.

"That depends on you, *Sensei*."

He slid his hands along the slippery fabric of her gown. "Tell me what you want, Stefanie."

This is it, she thought. "Tell me about Michael."

"Michael?" His voice was surprisingly cool and casual. "He's someone I was in the Navy with." He paused. "In Nam."

She was a child of the Vietnam War era herself and she recognized the impenetrable wall the code words "in Nam" were supposed to erect. She also knew that his lie concealed a more painful truth. Unless there were two Michaels, he simply wasn't willing to share something that was close to the heart of who and what he was.

She gently stroked his back, trying to pull his sadness out through her fingertips. "Do you want to tell me about him?" she asked. "If it gives you nightmares, maybe you should."

He covered her mouth with his. "Old war stories are boring," he said between kisses. "I don't want to let you get bored with me."

She rubbed her cheek against the softness of his beard. "You could never bore me."

She melted against him like a burning candle, her body responding instantly to his commands. Yet a part of her hovered over the bed and watched as they made love. There had been a chance for him to open up to her and he had refused it, and in his refusal she had sensed the solitary man behind the facade. He had been so willing to throw some light on the darkness of her fears and she longed to do the same for him. Her heart felt bruised by what she took as a lack of trust and it made it impossible for her to find the deepest pleasure in their union.

So she offered what he would accept, hoping he could soothe himself in the softness of her flesh, taking what solace he could find there until he trusted her enough to share his past.

* * *

I love you, he thought as he felt her body mold itself to his, her heart beating slowly and rhythmically against his back as she slept. *You're everything I never dared dream about.*

The nightmare about his brother had thrown him back to that time when he'd been stranded between rage and sorrow, unable to make his way to solid ground. In the five years since Patrolman Michael O'Connor had been murdered on a street corner in Boston, Dan doubted he'd spoken Michael's name aloud ten times. His years in Hollywood, which ended the same time as his brother's life, had faded like exposed film, but his unnecessary guilt over Michael was still sharp and clear.

Stefanie's arm was flung around his chest and he reached for her hand and pressed it over his heart. He hadn't been able to help his brother, but he had helped others since in a way that was both real and meaningful. He had taken Stefanie's fears and taught her to overcome them, showed her how to stand on her own again. He would like her now to stand alongside him. He might not be able to share his past, but he was eager to share his future.

The sensual glow of their weekend in New England lingered long after Stefanie returned to work on Monday. Now that she had a focus beyond Tele-Com/Conway, she found she had renewed interest in the minutiae of her job. Her boundaries had expanded once more; indeed, she felt capable and eager to do more than ever.

She was good at what she did and it had been ages since she'd taken simple pleasure in that fact. While it wasn't enough for her to build a life on, it could fill one portion of it adequately. She was glad, though, that Gabe Freeman was on vacation, because he would have been quick to spot the added *brio* she brought to each task and, she smiled to herself, equally quick to note the sparkle in her eyes and the reason for it.

She and Dan weren't able to see much of one another during the week. During the day she worked, and he taught at the Police Academy on a volunteer basis—a fact she often wondered about, but chalked up to making amends for a rough adolescence. In addition he ran afterhours self-defense classes for Long Island area businesses and ran classes at his school. Their time together was severely limited to late-night suppers at her apartment.

Maureen had followed up on her dinner invitation and, although they would have preferred spending the time alone, they both seemed to need to make their "official" family debut as a couple.

Before dinner Jim poured them glass after glass of Chianti and made Stefanie roar with laughter over Dan's exploits in the Navy. The stories about Dan's early attempts at learning the martial arts, funny as they were, also gave her some insight into the dedication this man she loved brought to every endeavor. Maureen, sipping Perrier in deference to her newly confirmed pregnancy, flitted in and out of the kitchen, depositing another platter of stuffed mushrooms on the cocktail table, replenishing the crudités, inserting a wisecrack here and there in the conversation.

Despite Dan's teasing about Maureen's culinary talents, the veal piccata was superb, and the dessert, a rich zabaglione, a delight. They lingered in the den afterward, enjoying the fire that crackled in the hearth and the conversation that warmed them all.

It was a little before 1:00 A.M. when Stefanie and Dan said good night and went upstairs to their room. The lamp on the dresser cast a soft gleam across the parquet floor and picked up the dusky rose tones in the Oriental carpet. As soon as the door closed behind them, he reached for her, pulling her close until her breasts flattened against his chest.

"Alone at last," he said with an exaggerated leer. "I found it hard to concentrate on anything but you tonight."

"Oh, really?" She tilted her head back and smiled up at him. "You seemed to concentrate pretty well on the veal and zabaglione, *Sensei.*"

His hands were doing wonderful things along her spine. "I couldn't hurt my sister's feelings now, could I? A family has to stick together."

"Well, I'm not family," she said, stroking his lower lip gently with her fingertip, "and I thought it was a great meal."

"You could become part of the family."

There was no special inflection given to his words, so for a second they didn't register with her. Then her eyes widened.

"Would you repeat that?" Her voice was a whisper. "I think I misunderstood you."

His dark blue eyes met hers. She held her breath.

"Will you marry me, Stefanie Colt?"

A thousand valid reasons why she should refuse bombarded her: They were so different; they'd known each other so short a time; they knew only the most basic things about each other. None of those reasons, however, could override the most valid reason why she should accept: She loved him.

"Stefanie?"

"This is so unexpected, Dan. Marriage is so—"

"Permanent?"

She nodded.

"'And I'm not a casual woman.'"

He quoted her words to him from their first ferry ride. "I'm not casual about marriage, Stefanie. I've known I wanted to live my life with you from that morning on the ferry." If asked, he could pinpoint the second when his future ceased to be his alone. He moved his lips closer to hers. "It seems I've forgotten one important thing: I love you." *More than I even knew*.

"Would you repeat that?" Her voice was soft and unbearably filled with promise.

"I love you."

He kissed her lips lightly, almost reverently. She felt suddenly like an awkward young girl rather than an adult woman of twenty-eight. She curled one hand around his neck and pulled his ear down to her mouth.

"I love you, *Sensei*," she murmured.

He kissed her throat, her shoulder. "I'm only your teacher in the *dojo*, Redhead."

"Oh, no, *Sensei*," she answered. "You have taught me well in other rooms."

He slid her creamy silk blouse off her shoulders and touched her breast through the lacy covering of her ivory bra.

Another lesson began.

Maureen and Jim were ecstatic, if not surprised, over Dan and Stefanie's engagement. There had been much hugging and kissing over the brunch table, along with a number of toasts to the expected baby and the impending wedding.

"The second you set a date, let me know," Maureen said as Stefanie got into the Porsche to leave. "I want to help you with everything I can."

"I promise, Mo," she said, leaning up to kiss her future sister-in-law's cheek. "As soon as we know, you'll know."

She felt light-headed from champagne and excitement. As Dan guided the car down the curved driveway and headed for the highway, she found herself babbling nonstop, her words a mixture of impressions and feelings she normally would have held back. He loved listening to her, even though some of it made no sense to him. However, at the center of her chatter, he heard a sense of envy over his family's positive reaction.

"When are you going to tell your family?" he asked as they approached the highway.

"I suppose I could phone them tonight." She didn't sound too sure.

"Isn't this the kind of thing you tell a family in person?"

Your family, perhaps, she thought but didn't say. How could she tell him that short of Prince Charles, no man's credentials were quite good enough for entry into the Colt clan. Even she, flesh-of-their-flesh, rarely measured up. "Well," she said finally, "I won't be going up until Thanksgiving."

He pulled over onto the shoulder of the right side of the road. He'd repeatedly sensed there was some kind of problem between her and her family. Delaying this announcement wouldn't do anyone any good at all. Although he wouldn't admit it even to himself, anxiety was beginning to gnaw at the back of his mind.

"Why not now?" he asked. She stared at him, mute as marble. "We're only an hour or so out of Boston."

For a few seconds she watched his face, her eyes brushing over the prominent cheekbones, the masculine cut of his jaw beneath the closely trimmed beard. "Well, they do all get together on Sundays for dinner."

He grinned. "And it is Sunday."

She grinned back, suddenly feeling like a mischievous kid who'd found the champagne punch. "And it is nearly dinner time…" She tossed her hands into the air. "What the hell? Let's do it!"

One hour and fifteen minutes later they turned onto the street where her parents lived.

"Are they having a convention here?" Dan asked as he parked on the street, two houses away.

Stefanie looked back at the crowd of cars.

"No," she said as he helped her out of the low-slung sports car. "This is an average Sunday at Chez Colt."

She took his arm as they walked up the flagstone path toward the front door. "This little Mercedes belongs to my mother; the Chrysler is my father's.'' She gestured farther up the driveway. "You remember Brendan's Corvette."

"You bet. It's the only car here I'd care to own."

She laughed. "Don't I know. The El Dorado belongs to Harrison and the Toronado belongs to Walker and Madolyn."

"Do we make our announcement now or wait till we're inside?"

She was still feeling silly from the champagne and playfully socked him in the arm.

"We might get a better reception from the cars, but I suppose we should go inside."

They stopped at the front door. Dan's nose was even with an enormous brass door knocker that probably cost as much as a year's rent did on the apartment he'd lived in as a boy. He had grown accustomed to having money, to expensive cars and large homes like Mo's, but these casual little touches, so natural to the old rich, still made him feel uneasy and out of synch.

Stefanie adjusted the bottom of her turquoise knit sweater over her cords, fixed the lapel on her blazer. She glanced at Dan in his open-necked plaid shirt, tight faded jeans, and leather jacket, and smiled.

Fasten your seat belt, Mother, she thought as she opened the front door. *It's going to be a bumpy night.*

"Are you nervous?" he asked, seeing the almost maniacal twinkle in her eyes.

"Not at all. We're announcing our engagement, not a guerrilla raid on Cuba," she lied.

She led him along the hallway. The heels on their boots clacked against the shiny dark wood floors. The dining room was empty. Only Myra, the cook, was there, piling dinner dishes on a large tray.

"Have they abandoned ship?" Stefanie asked, giving the woman a hug.

"Miss Stefanie!" Myra's smile creased her heavy lined face. "It sure is good to see you. I was saying to Annie the other day that we been missing you here for Sunday dinners."

Stefanie couldn't resist a glance at Dan. She giggled, whether from champagne or nerves, she didn't know. "I've been pretty busy, Myra."

The woman looked at Dan, obviously appraising him. A look passed between them that said she recognized him as one of her own. "So I see, miss," she said with laugh. "I'd be missing a few diners myself for such a handsome fellow." Myra nodded toward the library. "They're in there having dessert. I'll bring you both some coffee and my special coconut custard pie."

Stefanie took Dan's hand and led him from the dining room. The library was on the south side of the house, at the end of the enormous hallway. Dan's mouth suddenly felt dry and he wished he could have some water—with a lot of Scotch—to moisten it. Stefanie's eyes were glittering with excitement and the combination with her wavy red hair made her seem a little reckless but very desirable—different from the stiff-suited buisnesswoman he'd first met.

He stopped her about twenty feet from the door to the library.

"This might be a mistake," Dan said, nervously dragging his fingers through his hair. "I think I'd feel more comfortable in a suit. At least a sport coat." He motioned toward his leather jacket. "This doesn't exactly seem right for this place."

She looked up at him. "It's right for you normally, isn't it?"

"Yeah, normally," he said. "But I think I'd be more comfortable here if I were dressed differently."

"Nonsense." She brushed his concerns away with a wave of her hand. "Why should you be anyone but who you are?" She took his arm. "Come on." She didn't want him in a suit, she didn't want him in a shirt or tie. She wanted her staid old family to sit back on their heels and see that Brendan wasn't the only Colt with a mind of his own.

At first no one saw them when they entered the room. Harrison and Walker, both in blazers and turtlenecks, were standing near the bar with their mother, whose knit dress of silvered gray matched her hair. By the looks of intense concentration on their faces, Stefanie was sure they were talking business. Her father and Madolyn were sitting on the leather sofa, a pile of yellow papers spread between them. Brendan and Katie, a small woman with lovely chestnut hair, stood by the French doors looking like conspirators in an espionage plan. The only one missing was Harrison's wife, Mary, who was probably upstairs with the children.

Of course it was Brendan who finally noticed them.

"Red, Dan!" His voice was loud and happy as he and Katie hurried across the room to greet them. He kissed his sister, then shook Dan's hand.

"Dan, this is the famous Katie Keller," Stefanie said after she and the petite woman exchanged hugs.

Katie's level gray eyes smiled up at Dan. "Infamous Katie Keller is more like it." She gestured toward the others, who still hadn't made a move to greet Stefanie and Dan.

Brendan gave her a hug. "The folks think Katie is responsible for my fall from grace."

Katie laughed. "Little do they know Bren had already fallen long before I found him."

They bantered back and forth and Dan was beginning to feel less awkward when the rest of the family began its descent. He had an urge to back away, to set up a safe defensive distance the way he taught his students to do when faced with danger, and he had to remind himself he wasn't in a dark alleyway, but in the home of his fiancée's family. If he wasn't feeling so nervous, he would have found the situation laughable.

"You should have called, my dear." Elisabeth offered one powdered cheek to her daughter to kiss. "We would have set an extra plate for dinner."

"You're looking well, Mother," Stefanie said. She could feel her lighthearted mood sinking like a fencepost in wet cement.

"What brings you up here today?" Harrison inquired. Harrison was grooming himself for the position of patriarch, a post her father showed less and less interest in holding.

Dan felt invisible. They seemed either to look right through him or else their eyes lingered on his beard as if it harbored a communicable disease. How did a woman as passionate as his Stefanie come from such cold-blooded stock?

Beside him she took a deep breath. The champagne sparkle had faded and he could feel her nervousness in the way she clasped his hand with the trusting manner of a child afraid of the dark. They shouldn't have come, he thought. He shouldn't have pushed it.

"I'm glad you're all here," she began, praying she'd pick the right words. "This is Daniel O'Connor." She paused for a second, waiting for them to introduce themselves, shake his hand, something. The silence grew uncomfortably long. "Umm, I met Dan a few months ago when I took a self-defense course at his school."

"Self-defense?" This was her sister-in-law Madolyn. "You are taking karate?"

"Did something happen to you?" Her father, his attention finally piqued, entered the conversation.

She sighed. This was hardly the joyous celebration she had fantasized when the champagne had been crowding out reality. This was the way she'd always known it would be. She forced a small laugh.

"Well, listen, I'm not here to give you a lecture on self-defense. I—" she looked at Dan "—I mean, we want to let you be among the first to know that we're engaged to be married." Her last sentence came with the speed of a runner nearing the end of a grueling marathon.

If it hadn't been for Brendan and Katie and their genuine and exuberant display of happiness, Stefanie might have sunk to the expensive carpeting and cried like a forlorn child. Maureen and Jim had made their announcement into a celebration. Her family acted as if she'd announced she was buying a used car.

Harrison pulled her to one side. "Isn't this a little sudden?" he asked.

"Not at all," she said, rebellion coloring her voice. "We've known each other for quite a few months now."

"Where is he from?"

"Long Island."

"Not with that accent. Originally."

"Boston."

"Which part?"

"What do you want to hear, Harrison? Beacon Hill?"

She turned away from him. *Don't spoil this for me,* she thought. *Just once let me do something my way.*

Her father and Madolyn were making an attempt to draw Dan into conversation, while Brendan and Katie hovered around like protective mother hens. Elisabeth rang for Myra and asked for the champagne glasses.

"We have another announcement to make," she said, handing a bottle of Taittinger's to Harrison to open. "Besides Stefanie and Daniel's betrothal, Harrison has told me he plans to run for a seat in the House of Representatives next year."

The champagne cork popped and the rest of the family exploded into a rush of political fervor. Dan was left standing by the rolltop desk in the corner of the room, looking as out of place as she had always felt. Katie was talking to him and Stefanie could tell he was trying to be polite, but his dark blue eyes were curtained and he seemed far away.

She started toward him. Brendan, with a refill of champagne in his hand, put one arm around her.

"Don't look so sad, Red. Katie and I think it's terrific."

She sighed. "Don't let the rest of them hear you, little brother. You might be charged with collusion with the enemy."

Brendan snorted. "I was tried and found guilty years ago. I don't worry about it anymore."

To Stefanie it still hurt. They went over to Katie and Dan and jokingly made a toast to each other. Katie and Brendan teased about being in danger of losing their position as number one outcasts, but Stefanie found it hard to join in. Dan's discomfort seemed to flow right into her body and she was finding it hard to concentrate. Finally he picked up her left wrist and looked at her watch.

"We have a long drive ahead of us, kiddo," he said. "We should be hitting the road."

She slipped her arm into his and nodded. "We'll have to make our farewells."

"Think anyone will notice?"

Brendan and Katie chuckled, but Stefanie heard the tone in Dan's voice and recognized his intent. He meant every word.

"We're slipping out while you two make the rounds," Brendan said as he kissed her good-bye. "Be happy, Red," he whispered in her ear. "I like him."

Katie kissed Dan's cheek then embraced Stefanie. "Next time you guys go out to the Cape, please come and have dinner with us."

Stefanie, her arm firmly through Dan's, led the way across the library to where her father and Madolyn were huddled once again over their papers. Both were so preoccupied with talking about some aspect of Colt

Quarry that the good-byes were easy and painless. Walker was on the telephone and waved good-bye to them from the opposite side of the room. Elisabeth and Harrison were standing near the bar, talking intensely. As she led Dan over to them, she felt as if she were navigating her way through a field of land mines.

"Mother." Her voice sounded strange to her. "We have to be leaving." The inadequacies of her childhood tugged at her and she tried to push them away. "We both have work tomorrow and—well, it's a long drive home."

Elisabeth's eyes zeroed in on Dan. For the first time since she'd known him, Stefanie saw him break a stare and look away.

"Have you and my daughter set a date yet for your marriage?"

"No, Mrs. Colt, not yet."

Stefanie forced yet another laugh. "We only became engaged last night, Mother."

Her mother's eyes returned to Stefanie. "I sincerely hope neither one of you is entertaining the idea of marrying quickly." Elisabeth's voice was crisp as the drying leaves outside. "With Harrison's campaign starting up after the New Year, most of the family's energies will be focused on him. I'd prefer you to wait until after the election."

"If you don't mind, Mrs. Colt, Stefanie and I will marry when it suits us." In the quiet of the library his voice sounded more wrong-side-of-town than it had when he lived there.

Elisabeth's eyebrows arched elegantly toward her hairline. Stefanie's ulcer burned under her rib cage and she hurried to smooth things over.

"What Dan means is, we'll have to work our wedding around our schedules, Mother. But we'll take your thoughts into consideration."

Dan, who had said exactly what he meant to say, was angered by her conciliatory manner. He'd always thought of Stefanie as a fighter, with him she'd always been ready to give as good as she got. Initially it was her feistiness that had attracted him to her. But with her mother he had seen her shrink until she was a small child standing next to him, clutching his hand for support. He hated what they did to her and he also hated to admit that Elisabeth had the same effect on him. Two minutes in that library and he was a tough kid once again, checking out the silverware, looking for a wallet to lift. He knew he had come a long way with his life—had, in fact, completely turned it around. Yet someone like Elisabeth Colt could speak to him without words. *I can see through you, boy,* her look said. *I know who you really are.*

Elisabeth offered a cheek to her daughter for a good-bye kiss, then inclined her head in Dan's direction. "Will you both be joining us for Thanksgiving?"

Stefanie nodded. "Probably." She didn't turn to Dan to ask him, and his anger intensified. "I'll call you next week about it."

Dan was quiet as they closed the front door after them and walked down the driveway toward the Porsche parked at the curb a few houses down. Was he invisible or did her family just possess the uncanny talent for making him feel so? He felt as if his body were coiled tight as a mainspring and the slightest thing could make him pop. He hated the way her mother had made him feel—as if he carried an invisible film of lower middle class mores with him still. But, even more than that, he hated seeing Stefanie bend before a woman who apparently didn't give a damn about her. In those few minutes in that library he had seen her slip away from him, slip back into the fold of her family. She wanted so much to be loved by them that it hurt him physically because he knew that what she needed they could never provide.

They were quiet as they rolled down the Massachusetts Turnpike south toward New York. Stefanie, who had been watching Boston and the environs slip past her window, sighed softly then turned to him. She placed her hand gently on his leg and he felt a jolt of pure lust hit him square in the gut. Signaling, he pulled off the highway and onto the shoulder of the road. Her eyes were wide, visible even in the darkened car. The passing headlights of other vehicles cast stripes of light across her face that flickered like an old-time movie. Without a word he reached for her. She had her seat belt fastened and it tugged against her chest as he pulled her closer, the stick shift acting as a barrier between them.

"Dan—" she managed, placing her hand flat on his chest and pushing him slightly away so she could catch her breath. "What on earth—?"

His hands slid over her face and neck and breasts as he kissed her again. He had a sudden vision of her drifting away from him, behind a barrier he could never climb. It terrified him.

"I want you," he said. He would make the power of his love and desire push back the demons that had come between them so suddenly.

"And I want you." She sounded puzzled. "But not here. Not like this."

"We'll get a room."

She stared at him. "For an hour?"

"For as long as we want it," he answered as he guided the Porsche back toward town for the second time that night.

12

Stefanie was curled on her office sofa, her stockinged feet tucked beneath her, her face nestled against Dan's chest. "Come to my apartment after your seminar tonight," she said. "I'll have something warm waiting for you."

He stroked her hair. "Yourself, I hope."

She chuckled. "I was thinking more along the lines of a quiche."

He slid one finger between the buttons of her black crepe de chine blouse and touched the rise of her breast. "I think we should set a date, Stefanie." He had been pushing this for the two weeks they'd been engaged. "There doesn't seem to be much of a reason for us to wait."

She hesitated. Their unexpected lovemaking the Sunday night they announced their engagement had set her slightly off-balance, as if the world had tilted just a bit and she was in danger of slipping off the edge. Dan had been like a man possessed as he tried to blot out her consciousness with his kisses, to wipe away her past with his body. That interlude with her family had disturbed her less than ever before; having Dan by her side had made her feel stronger. She had the sense, though, that something about it had disturbed him greatly; but when she questioned him about it, he shrugged it off as if it didn't matter at all. Time and again she had seen him ignore his own pain in order to ease the pain inside her, and each time it left her feeling useless. He refused to let her become a part of his interior life the way he was a part of hers.

Now he wanted to set a date for their wedding.

"An engagement period can be a lovely thing," she said slowly. "Besides, you've never seen me in a really foul mood. You may want to reconsider."

He could feel her hesitation in every fiber of his body. *You're coming on too strong.* "You've never seen me in one either. Would it make you call off a marriage?"

"Depends on how cranky you were." She smiled at him but he didn't smile back. His blue eyes grew dark, distant. "I'm only teasing, Dan. There's nothing on earth that could stop me from loving you."

"Then why wait? Why don't we just get the blood tests done, get the license, and get married. I don't want a big production, do you?"

She shook her head. "Not at all. But I have the Hawaii trip coming up on Monday, and I won't be back until the following Sunday after Thanksgiving. That would put us into early December."

"Can't someone else make the trip for you? Freeman, maybe?"

"No." Her voice was firm. "This is my responsibility and I've shirked it far too long." She kissed the side of his mouth. "You're to blame, you know. If it hadn't been for your classes, I never would have the nerve to do it."

"Terrific." He looked disgusted.

"You're acting like a little boy, Dan. We'll get married when I come back."

"When?"

She did some quick calculations. "How about December fifteenth?"

He grinned. "How about the fifth?"

"Compromise on the tenth?"

"You've got a deal." He shook her hand, then bent forward and nuzzled his face against the skin exposed by the V neck of her blouse. He undid one button.

She sat up straighter and gently pushed him away. "Dan—anybody could walk in."

"Don't worry," he said, rebuttoning her blouse and grinning at the sight of her nipples tightening against the thin fabric. "I won't compromise you, Ms. Colt." His face seemed to darken with passion. "I just want you to be thinking of me this afternoon. I want you to be thinking of all the things we'll do to make each other happy tonight."

Her body tingled at his words. She walked him downstairs and out to his car in the visitors' parking lot behind the building. He unlocked the door to the Porsche, then reached to kiss her good-bye. She stepped back, striking an exaggerated self-defense posture.

"Come here," he said. "Let me kiss you good-bye."

She grinned at him, keeping her safe distance between them. "Sorry, *Sensei*. Haven't you heard? Anticipation is part of the game."

With a cheery wave of her hand she turned and headed back toward the office, relishing the fact that she had turned the tables on him.

However, he did turn out to be right. For the rest of the afternoon, Stefanie found herself drifting in and out of romantic and erotic daytime dreams about the nighttime pleasures to come. Even the pile of paperwork she had to plow through in preparation for her Hawaii trip on Monday didn't faze her. She was still hard at work at seven when Gabe came in to say goodbye and give her a little bon voyage gift his wife Eileen had picked out. It was well after nine o'clock when she finally took her plane tickets out of her desk, dug out her hotel reservation confirmation slip, grabbed all the files and photos she'd be needing, and tossed them into her briefcase. She'd given the extra push because she really wanted to take the next day, Friday, off to run last-minute errands she'd been postponing.

When she got home, she threw a frozen diet dinner in the oven, then relaxed in a warm tub of scented water, listening to an FM radio station that played all the songs of her youth. Nowadays she understood everything those old sweet songs had to say in a way she hadn't understood as a girl. The high poignant sounds of Smokey Robinson, the vibrating intensity of the early Linda Ronstadt, any and all of the girl groups from Motown and their clarion calls to the power of love: It was all aimed directly at her heart. It would all be so perfect if Dan would just open up to her and share his feelings, his past.

She sighed and leaned back in the tub, letting the waters lap around her breasts and throat. *He will,* she thought. *Just give him time.*

Dan had been riding high after the seminar that evening. His words had met their mark and he'd left every rookie cop in the auditorium thinking seriously about new ways to defuse crowd violence. When Captain Harron took him aside afterward, he'd been preparing himself to modestly accept the man's compliments.

What he'd never expected was to discover that the woman he loved had hired a private investigator to dig around and ask questions about his background.

"That detective's not too sharp," Harron had said, shaking his head. "One of the guys in the hostage unit heard what he was up to, and he got a friend at division level to collect what info the guy's got on you and stop him from getting any more."

The invasion of his privacy angered Dan. "I've done nothing to be ashamed of, Jack," he said. "I was a little wild but you know all about me."

Harron nodded. The police had done a very thorough check before bringing Dan into their fold. The captain cleared his throat. "Have you told your fiancée about your arrest record?"

Dan shook his head. "I haven't even thought of it—it was so long ago that I forget sometimes. I was just a kid." He looked at the older man. "I suppose I should," he said. "I don't want her to be surprised if this gets out or think it's more than it was."

Harron's large brown eyes seemed sadder than usual. "Danny—" He hesitated but knew he had to tell him. "The detective was hired by Stefanie Colt."

Dan stopped at a red light after hours of aimless driving and touched the folded pieces of paper in his breast pocket, then took a drag on the cigarette that burned in the car's ashtray. He hadn't smoked in ten months but tonight it had seemed like the right time to start again.

He turned onto Stefanie's street.

Inside the apartment Stefanie was debating between calling every hospital emergency room between there and Montauk or jumping into her car and looking for Dan herself. He had said he'd be there around nine o'clock, but here it was well after midnight and he hadn't even called. Anger and fear battled inside her and she found it impossible to concentrate on anything at all.

She paced the living room, twisting her hands. Suddenly the doorbell rang. She stopped dead in her tracks, then, as if awakening from a dream, she flew to the door and opened the locks.

"Dan! I was so worried! I—" She was about to throw herself into his arms and weep with relief but he stepped away from her and into the living room. As he passed, she could smell Scotch and cigarette smoke and prickles of apprehension popped out on her arms and legs.

"Did you have car trouble?" she asked.

"No."

She followed him into the living room. Everything about him seemed different. He was wearing the dark suit that he saved for business meetings, and he seemed to be holding himself at an odd angle. His spine was unnaturally straight, stiff and unyielding. He seemed a stranger to her.

"Do you have any Scotch?"

She shook her head. "Let me make some coffee."

His eyes met hers for the first time since he arrived. "I'm not drunk, Stefanie," he said. "Not yet."

He went over to the bar near the stereo and found the bottle of Dewar's on the top shelf. She perched on the sharp arm of her sofa, her ulcer burning.

"Something's wrong," she said. "I can tell."

He looked up at her and took a slug of booze. "Playing detective again, Stefanie?"

She shivered slightly. This angry dark stranger wasn't the Dan she knew.

"What are you talking about, Dan? I don't understand."

He walked around the bar and came toward her. He reached into the pocket of his jacket, pulled out a folded pile of papers, then tossed them at her.

"I'm surprised you made such a lousy choice in detectives. You could have found someone better—with your money." She said nothing, just stared at him, clutching the typed sheets. "You could have gotten someone first rate. Magnum, P.I." He laughed unpleasantly. "He got a few things wrong, by the way. I'm a hundred eighty pounds, not one eighty-five." His eyes narrowed. "All in the interest of accuracy, you understand."

Her heart pulsed in her throat and swallowing was almost impossible. "I don't know what you're talking about."

"He hasn't given you his report yet?" He motioned toward the papers in her hands. "See what I mean? He's just not on top of things. Consider those an advance copy."

She stood up and the papers fell to the carpet. Some of them drifted under the sofa, the chairs.

"Someone investigated you?"

He drained the Scotch and put the empty glass down on the end table. "Cut the innocent act, Stefanie. Spare us both."

Her breathing became more rapid and she could feel adrenaline flow in response to her anger. "Why would you believe I'd do something like that?"

He bent and sifted through the scattered papers then pulled one out. He stood up and read: "The A. Danvers Investigative Services Company, Garden City, New York. Client: Stefanie Louise Colt. Address: Twenty-seven B Sycamore. Apartment One B. Marked paid." He tossed it back on the floor. "Why don't you read it while I have another Scotch? I'll be happy to fill in the blanks before I leave."

She was still staring down at the papers that bore her name. Her mind was fuzzy; shock and rage numbed her ability to think.

"I don't want to read it," she said. "I would never have done this to you, Dan. Don't you know me better than that?"

He grunted as he poured more Scotch into his tumbler.

Suddenly a vision of her brother Harrison and his pointed questions the night they announced their engagement swept down on her. She could see his cold pale eyes, feel the sharp edges of his suspicious mind scratching against her. "Harrison," she said. "Harrison would do something like this."

Dan looked up from his drink. "Come on, Stefanie. Don't blame your family for this. You had questions about me. Plenty of them. Admit it."

"Of course I had questions, damn it! But I figured you would answer them for me one day. I'd never hire a detective to get the answers for me."

He pointed at the papers again. "You really should read those. There's some pretty juicy stuff in there about when I was in the Navy. You could feed all your upper-class fantasies." He stopped for a moment. "Tell me—was I the first guy you slept with who didn't have a PhD after his name?"

"You disgust me." Her hand ached to slap him. She wanted to hurt him for reducing what they'd had into something common, sordid.

"Can't stand the truth, Ms. Colt? Couldn't any of your Boston bluebloods make you feel the way I did? I bet you never made that low growl for them like you did for—"

"Shut up!" Her hands had automatically reached up to cover her ears. "What is it you want to hear? You were the best lover I've ever had—does that satisfy you? Sex was the best thing we had going. Maybe my next lover will be a martial arts instructor." She stopped because she was close to tears. "Are you satisfied now, Dan? Now we've said things we won't be able to forget."

"Don't worry," he answered. "When I walk out of here tonight, I'll have forgotten all of this. Believe me."

She'd lost him; she could see it. She'd gone too far, said too much. There was nothing she could say that could erase the doubts someone had deliberately planted in his heart.

"You're not being fair," she said. "I shouldn't have to come to you like a penitent begging forgiveness for something I never did."

He drained his second Scotch. "You're losing your touch, Colt. You missed another chance to give me a vocabulary lesson. Maybe I don't know what a penitent is."

Her face burned at the memory of that moment in her office. "Okay!" All semblance of control was gone. "I'm guilty! I'm guilty of being born into money. I'm guilty of going to the right schools. I'm guilty of every lousy thing you think I'm guilty of!" *I'm guilty of loving you too much.*

He heard the words "I'm guilty," and the fierce pain that ripped at his insides like a wild thing trying to escape drowned out all other words. He wanted to smash everything in the room, howl with rage that the most wonderful thing in his life had disappeared before his very eyes. He hated Harron for telling him, he hated her family for being who they were, hated the world that destroyed everything good.

"Too bad he screwed up, Stefanie." Why did she just watch him like that with those green eyes of hers so open, so vulnerable? She was nothing like that at all. "If he'd done a better job, I might never have found out. You could still have the fun of hitting the sack with someone without initials after his name."

"Right now I can't believe I ever let you near me."

"Well, you did," he said, "and I know you'll never be able to forget how I made you feel."

He picked up his car keys from the credenza and went to leave.

"Wait a minute." Her voice was pure fire. Rage had tempered her hurt and forged a new strength. "You're right, Dan—sex with you was incredible. I'll probably never find another lover like you." He flinched and she was pleased to know she could hurt him as he hurt her. "But, Dan, maybe that's all it was—sex. Did you ever let me close to you—really close to you? Did you ever let me share your feelings? You wouldn't even let me comfort you when you had that nightmare about Michael." She paused for a minute. She was losing it. Her pain was starting to overpower the strength of anger, and pain weakened her position, made her vulnerable to him once again.

"You want to know about Michael? Read all about him, lady. You paid for the privilege."

"Damn you! Do you have to be the strong one all the time? Don't you think just once I would have liked the opportunity to share your troubles, to help you?" Her voice was beginning to break. She stopped abruptly. She gestured toward the papers. "I don't want to read anything about you, Dan. Nothing at all." All of her strength seemed to be leaching out of her and she leaned against the back of an armchair for support.

"You know, I'm glad it happened," she said. "Really. If you can believe I'm capable of this, then—" She stopped. She was simply too tired, too far gone to say anymore. "Go." She looked across the room at the man who would always have her heart. "I can't bear to look at you anymore."

He didn't want to leave her. He wanted to say, "Hold me in your arms. Make me believe you." But her words had been deadly and they had been well-aimed.

He went to the front door and opened it, then turned and looked at her for a moment, his eyes taking in every detail of her face and form.

She had steeled herself, expecting him to slam the door behind him. Instead he closed it softly and somehow the sound seemed more final, more heartbreaking than she could have imagined possible.

But hadn't he taught her as much? Softness was always the deadlier force.

"Ah, *Sensei*," she said aloud as she locked the door against the world outside. "How right you were."

No matter what she did she couldn't get warm again. The shivering that started when Dan showed up had intensified, and now, three hours later, she was huddled in the corner of her sofa, a blanket around her shoulders, and a cold anger in her heart.

Her mind was closed to Dan. She couldn't let herself think about him or all they had lost that night. Someday, in a future she found hard to believe would exist, she would deal with the fact he had believed her capable of such an act. She would also have to deal with the fact that many of his accusations had been very close to the bone.

Now, though, her brother Harrison was uppermost in her mind. This whole shoddy incident was marked with his touch. He was so avid for a seat in the House that he would let nothing, and no one, stand in his way. Her first thought had been that her mother was involved in this, but the underhanded way things had been managed was totally unlike her mother's more direct style.

She had tried to sleep but found it impossible. Anger-fueled adrenaline kept her heart pounding inside her chest until she felt bruised from within. *Fight or flight* they called the phenomenon.

All her life she'd taken flight from any real confrontation with her family.

She got up and grabbed the Suffolk county phone directory from her desk drawer, flipped it open to the listing of commuter airlines. The number for the shuttle to Boston was circled in red.

This time she was going to fight.

The offices of Colt, Colt, McKenzie and Colt were spacious, elegant, and terribly, terribly quiet. The walls were so thick, the floors so densely carpeted, that sound was absorbed without a trace.

Elisabeth was in court, the receptionist said, and Harrison was on the telephone, so the woman motioned Stefanie to have a seat while she waited. Stefanie wanted to kick in the heavy oak door to his office, but instead she sat primly on the edge of her chair, ankles crossed, hands folded on her lap, and quietly burned. Creating a scene in the waiting room—exciting as it sounded—would only ruin her chances of getting through to Harrison.

Finally the receptionist ushered Stefanie into his office. He stood up when she came in and pulled a small armchair over near his desk. He waited until she sat down before lowering himself into his enormous leather swivel chair.

Ever since she could remember, Harrison had been scrupulously polite; he was the kind of man who would plunge a knife in your back then offer to pay your dry-cleaning bill. Now he leaned back in his chair and put his hands behind his head, and she saw the beginnings of a middle-aged belly straining the buttons of his Oxford-cloth shirt. She waited for him to speak.

"Well, Stefanie, are you here to volunteer for the campaign?" The expression in his pale blue eyes was obscured by the half-lensed glasses he'd begun to wear recently.

She ignored his question. Instead she opened her pocketbook and pulled out the report Dan had presented her with last night. Harrison looked puzzled, a little amused, as she pushed the papers across his desk toward him. He was smiling as he picked them up.

"What's all this?"

She stared at him, her features like the granite her family had founded their fortunes upon. "Why don't you tell me?"

He riffled through the typed sheets with the air of a parent indulging a wayward child, then he looked up at her over the half-moons of glass that rested on his nose.

"I see you had your doubts about your boyfriend yourself."

She had to hand it to him: He was a cool liar.

"You'll do well in politics, Harrison. If I didn't know better, I'd believe you."

He pointed to her name on the top sheet of paper. "It says right here you commissioned the work."

"I know," she said. "I'd like to know how you managed that."

"Yes, Harrison. Tell us how you managed it."

Stefanie turned around and saw Elisabeth standing in the doorway. Harrison, a junior partner, jumped to his feet and offered his chair to his mother. She refused it and sat on the leather sofa.

Elisabeth looked at her daughter; Stefanie met her gaze without looking away.

"Someone used my name and hired a detective to investigate Dan's background. I think it was Harrison who did it."

Her mother looked at her son, who stood near the computer terminal behind his desk. "You fool," she said. "Why did you do it?"

Harrison hesitated. "It should be pretty clear, especially to you, Mother. Her boyfriend was the X factor in the campaign." He spread his hands in front of him. "I needed information but I didn't want to be involved."

Elisabeth frowned, then smoothed the furrows on her brow with two fingers. "That's absurd. Why didn't you use a pseudonym? It's common knowledge Stefanie is your sister."

Harrison shifted as if his clothes had suddenly shrunk a half-size. "The detective made a clerical error and—"

"Liar," Stefanie interrupted. The real truth suddenly became clear to her. "This is exactly what you wanted to have happen, isn't it? That detective wasn't a fool, an incompetent—he followed your instructions to the letter. You wanted this to leak to Dan so it would break us up.''

His silence confirmed it.

''I had asked Stefanie to postpone any marriage plans until after the election next year,'' Elisabeth said. ''This was totally unnecessary.''

Harrison turned his pale gaze on his mother. ''I heard that and I also heard him tell you it was none of your business. That guy is too hot-tempered; he could wreck my campaign in a second.'' He grabbed the papers from the desk and pushed them toward his mother. ''Damned good thing I did this—he has a prison record.''

Elisabeth looked over at her daughter; her gray eyes were unreadable. ''Is this true?''

Stefanie silently blessed Maureen and her gift of gab. ''He was seventeen years old, Mother. It was while he was grieving for his father.''

Elisabeth looked at her son, then back at her only daughter. ''In a political campaign, Stefanie, the candidate isn't the only one under public scrutiny. His entire family is under the microscope as well. Perhaps Harrison was just—''

Stefanie was having none of it. ''I suppose you have a dossier on everyone in this family?''

Harrison looked at her. ''Our family's background is an open book.''

''The sainted Colts. I forgot. How about Mary and Madolyn? Do they measure up?''

''They both come from old and respected families.''

''And there's the rub,'' Stefanie said. ''Dan was born on the wrong side of the Charles.''

Harrison chose to ignore the sarcasm. "His family checked out quite well, actually. In fact, he had a brother who—"

"Spare me," she said angrily. "Anything I'll learn about my in-laws, I'll learn firsthand." She didn't want him to know how well his plan had succeeded.

"I have no problem with your in-laws. It's Daniel. You could have told us about his prison record."

Hold on. Don't let them see they've gotten to you.

"It's none of your business, Harrison. It's in the past." She shook her head. "I had no idea my family was into KGB tactics."

"KGB?" Harrison laughed. "Are you part of the real world, Stefanie, or are you still in the nineteenth century? This is common practice." He paused then aimed his next shot. "Didn't you take a lie detector test when you started with Tele-Com?"

"Yes, and I objected to it. But, Harrison!" Her voice grew louder. "This is *family* we're talking about. Family."

"He's not our family." Harrison stood up.

Stefanie recognized his attempt to intimidate her so she stood up also, their eyes on a level.

"He will be."

"That's what I'd like to talk about. I'd like you to reconsider your plans to marry him."

Her breath held for a second, then she exhaled in a loud, harsh laugh. "I'd like to ask you to reconsider running for Congress."

Elisabeth gasped.

"You can't mean that," Harrison said.

"But I do." She wanted to wrap her arms across her chest to protect herself from the pain she felt, but she thought of Dan and all he'd taught her. Instead she straightened up and stared at her brother.

"You're talking about my political career."

"And you're talking about the rest of my life."

Her mother cleared her throat. "It's hardly the same thing, my dear."

Stefanie stared at her mother as if twenty-eight years of illusion had been swept aside.

"You're right, Mother. It's not. It's much more important." She turned and included Harrison in her speech. "Both of you have careers and families. All I wanted was the same privilege." She'd slipped and she prayed no one noticed. Her mother's eyes were focused on her hands, which rested on her lap. Harrison, however, was not through.

"Live with him if you have to. Just don't make him part of this family."

She bent down and gathered up her coat and purse. "I wouldn't dream of making him part of this family. I only wish I could have become part of his."

She didn't wait for a response. Instead she lifted her chin high and strode out of the office, across the reception area, and out the door. She didn't slow down and she didn't break until she reached the elevator banks. She punched the down button, then leaned her head against the wall and let the tears flow. Suddenly she felt a hand on her shoulder and, quickly wiping her cheeks, she turned and saw Elisabeth standing next to her.

"I'm sorry, Stefanie." For the first time Stefanie could remember, Elisabeth looked her age. Each of her sixty-nine years were visible in the network of lines around her mouth. They seemed more deeply etched than they had just weeks ago.

"I don't know what I can say, Mother."

"You and Daniel are no longer engaged?"

The elevator door opened. Stefanie hesitated for a second then let it pass.

"We're no longer engaged," she said finally. "You can all breathe a collective sigh of relief."

"Do I seem that heartless to you?"

"At times, yes." Stefanie felt an enormous sadness over the chasm that had always separated mother and daughter.

Elisabeth laid a gnarled hand on her daughter's arm in an awkward and unnatural gesture. "It has always been very difficult for me to show affection."

"I know, Mother." She thought of her childhood when hugs and comfort had come from housekeepers and nannies. "I wish it could have been different between us."

Elisabeth nodded. "As do I. Harrison and Walker I could manage. But you and Brendan—" She sighed. "You two were like little monkeys clinging to me, demanding love and attention, and—" She stopped and for a second her strong shoulders sagged. "I'd been in my career for too long. I was too old to learn new ways. I'm sorry if I failed you."

Tears choked Stefanie but she could only nod at her mother. She couldn't comfort her.

"Is there hope for you and your young man?"

Stefanie shook her head. "No. He believes I initiated the investigation, and even if I could convince him otherwise, would he be welcome in this family?"

"I can't speak for anyone else," Elisabeth said, "but I would welcome him if you loved him enough."

In twenty-eight years, Elisabeth had never shown emotion like that in front of her daughter, and it moved Stefanie despite her pain and anger.

"I love you, Mother."

Elisabeth's head jerked up and she stared at her daughter, unable to dissemble. "Thank you," she said quietly.

Stefanie pushed for another elevator. "I don't know that love's enough, though. So much has happened between us."

"I know," Elisabeth said. "And I'm too old to change."

They were quiet. The elevator rumbled its way up to their floor, then the door creaked open.

"Take care, Mother."

She got into the elevator. Elisabeth watched as the doors slowly closed and Stefanie saw her mother mouth the words "I love you."

Hawaii hurt Stefanie's eyes. Everything about the island was too much: It was too sunny, too vivid with color, even the air was too sweet with the scent of orchids and ginger blossoms and plumeria. It assaulted her with a sensuality so blatant and unabashed that she found herself aching from the inside out for Dan's touch.

Anger toward her family had kept her sorrow over their breakup at bay, but the second she got off the plane and found herself in the middle of a paradise designed for lovers, she fell deep into an abyss of loneliness and regret. Her temper had gotten away from her. Dan had been deeply hurt and angry. She had to admit she would have felt the same if the tables had been turned. It was hard for her to face it, but some of his remarks had been unpleasantly true.

She had been, in fact, initially attracted to him because he represented something that was totally alien to her upbringing. Maybe it was postadolescent rebellion or something—she didn't know—but the strong sexual current between them had been fueled at first by the fact that he was everything she thought her family would despise. It wasn't until she got to know him that she realized his tough exterior hid a soul with a goodness and gentleness that only the very strong possessed.

When she got to her hotel, she impulsively placed a long distance call to Dan but only got the answering machine. "Dan, it's Stefanie. I—" She sounded like a fool. What could she possibly say to a machine that could make a difference? She hung up.

Every morning the company limo came at seven and carried her off to the Conway installation on the windward side of the island of Oahu. Then, each evening around six, it would deposit her back on the doorstep of the Prince Kuhio Hotel and the tall white-haired man who served as major domo/concierge would shake his head in dismay as he watched the sad-eyed *haole* cross the lobby toward the elevator.

The Conway people kept her busy evenings with dinner invitations to touristy luaus and little-known local haunts, and she found the activity helped her mind steer clear of Dan for at least a few seconds every day. One of the vice presidents even whisked her to his home on Kauai for Thanksgiving Hawaiian-style with his family. It was lovely, but her thoughts strayed back home and she wished with all her heart things could have been different.

The company held a big opening celebration on her last night in Hawaii, and she was exhausted the next morning when she boarded the jumbo jet for the long trip home. Including the stopover in Los Angeles, she would be airborne, or at least traveling, for twelve hours, and with the changing time zones she would not arrive in New York until the following morning. The thought itself was exhausting, and once the plane took off, she curled up in her seat and tried to sleep.

She couldn't settle down for a long time, however, and it wasn't until they were nearing Los Angeles that she finally dropped off into a deep sleep.

"Miss." Someone was shaking her. Her eyes fluttered open and focused on the attendant next to her. "We've landed at LAX for a one-hour stopover. You can get up and stretch your legs, if you like."

She managed a smile. "Thanks, but I think I'll stay on and get some sleep."

A number of passengers got off, many of whom were at their final destination. It was dark outside her window, and the lights of Los Angeles twinkled in the distance. She closed her eyes, trying to ignore the sounds of new passengers boarding the red-eye to New York.

She drifted off to sleep again, hardly bothered by the roaring of the engines as the plane took off, or by the crazy angle of the cabin as it gained altitude. She was deep in a dream, a dream about softness and strength, of arms that would protect, and she didn't want to emerge.

The morning after their argument Dan went up to the Cape. He called Mike and left him in charge of the school and, tossing a few things into the minuscule trunk of the Porsche, fled to the mind-numbing monotony of the highways in an effort to escape the sense of desolation that embraced him.

He spent the days walking up and down the empty beach, gazing for hours on end at the restless gray ocean. He either ate soup from cans or drank coffee by the pot, not caring about taste or sustenance. Being awake was torture because Stefanie was on his mind constantly, but being asleep was worse because the nightmare had returned.

Each and every night since he broke up with her, he had suffered through it, been blinded by the imagined sight of his brother dropping to the ground, a bullet wound in his stomach, blood staining the uniform and dripping onto the slush on the sidewalk. Dan's subconscious was able to recreate, in graphic detail, what he had not been there to see. The bullet exploded behind his eyes and he felt the force of the shot, felt all of Michael's fears and loneliness.

He would throw himself out of bed, his breathing as labored as if he'd been running for hours. If he'd only taken time to show Michael some of his techniques. But, no. He'd been too busy in Hollywood, too busy teaching some bleached-blond muscle-brains to take a punch, that he hadn't bothered to show his brother how to stay alive.

It had taken him five years to prove to himself that he was worth something, that what he could do mattered. Nothing would ever being Michael back, but there was some satisfaction in seeing that it didn't happen to someone else, that he had kept one more person safe. If nothing else, he had at least seen the change in Stefanie—she had literally blossomed before his eyes.

She'd tried to tell him she didn't hire the detective and he wanted to believe her; however, the tough kid who cried out for love wouldn't buy it.

And now the man suffered.

So, when Elisabeth Colt called him, after getting his Cape Cod number from the detective's report, Dan's first instinct was to tell her to go to hell. But he had detected a note of sadness in her voice and, in the end, agreed to meet her in Boston that evening for drinks.

He'd been nervous at first—his tie felt like a noose around his neck. But Elisabeth had surprised him. She was blunt, sometimes unkind, but she was honest and he appreciated that. She explained what had happened, not sparing herself in the telling, and he found himself gaining a grudging respect for this stiff-backed, sad woman who sat in front of him. Who was he to judge a woman who found sharing her inner self to be impossible, when he had withheld his deepest needs from Stefanie?

Elisabeth said Stefanie loved him. She also said that if he was half the man she thought he was, he would take the first plane out and force her to listen to him, force himself to try again despite the pain.

He spent the entire night driving up and down the length of the Cape, his mind a tangle of fears and dreams. Around four in the morning he suddenly turned his car around and headed back to New York. He never knew why, but instead of heading first toward the school as he usually did he went to his apartment and saw the red light blinking on his tape machine. He flipped it on and heard her voice.

By eleven o'clock he had reached Gabe Freeman, found out when her flight would be leaving Hawaii. He would meet her at L.A. and fly home with her. Maybe in the darkness and quiet of the night flight they could discover if there were anything left for them.

Suddenly Stefanie realized she wasn't dreaming. Her nostrils twitched at the tang of leather and spice and the scent that belonged to one person on earth. She looked up, brushing her hair from her eyes, and stared at Dan.

"I'm dreaming. You can't be here."

"I am." His smile was tentative.

Even in the darkened cabin she could see he was no mirage.

"I don't understand. Why? How?"

"A very wise woman told me if I was half the man she thought I was, I would come to you and try to work things out."

"Maureen?"

He smiled at her. "Your mother."

She was wide awake now. "My mother?"

"One and the same." He shook his head. "I have to say she's one hell of a lady, Stefanie. Underneath all that starch she's a damned fine woman."

"I don't understand any of this. I can't believe—"

"But I can. I know your brother hired the detective," he interrupted. "I guess I always believed it deep down. I was just so angry, so—" He stopped. The fact was, the memories of his earlier life had engulfed him and stripped him of logic. "I can only say I'm sorry." He dragged his hand through his hair in the gesture she remembered so well that her heart ached. She longed to touch him. "I don't know if this makes any difference to you now," he said. "I don't know if what we had can survive."

She heard the tremor in his voice and her heart broke with love for him. "Can it?" she asked. "We said some terrible things."

"I know." He watched her face, where love, sorrow, gratitude, and rage all battled for dominance. "I said a lot of things, Stefanie. A lot of low, lousy things I didn't mean."

She felt the tremor in his fingers. She shook her head gently. "You meant some of them, Dan."

He stared at her. Was it really over after all?

"That was probably the first time we were totally straight with one another." She kept her green eyes focused on him so he could see everything she was feeling as she spoke. "You were even right about some of it. A big part of this for me was the element of danger. You were forbidden fruit." She smiled at him. "But when I got to know you, I realized you were so much more. You stopped being a symbol of my past, a symbol of something I'd never have the guts to be, and you started being the man I love."

"What is it you can never be?" Dan asked. His heart was pounding so crazily in his chest he could barely speak.

"I thought I could never be as free as you, as sure of myself. Confident enough to choose a position in life and defend it."

He laughed for the first time. "You never had any trouble defending your position with me."

"I know." Stefanie's voice was soft, reflective. "That's because you allowed me to be who and what I am. You never forced me to be something I wasn't."

"That's not what you said in the *dojo.*" There was hope for them. There had to be.

"Even there," she said, her voice serious. "Even there you saw me as a full individual. With you there was the freedom of fight."

"We've had our share of 'discussions,'" he said with a rueful grin.

"And we'll have more." Her words were almost lost in the roar of the plane's engines.

Dan put an arm gently around her and drew her as close as the seat rest would allow. "Can we have a future, Stefanie? Can we start again?"

"You tell me," she countered. "You know so much of me. All my hopes and fears have been paraded in front of you. I know next to nothing about you." She listed the items on her fingers. "All you ever told me was you liked Michael Jackson's music, Al Pacino's movies, Irish whiskey—which I've never seen you drink—and Italian food. A wife should really know more about her husband than that, don't you think?''

His heart soared. He understood this was her way of telling him the papers had remained unread. They had existed, she could have satisfied her curiosity, yet her sense of integrity and her love for him had prevailed over her anger and enabled her to respect his privacy. He loved her more at that moment than he could have imagined possible.

He called a flight attendant over and asked for two glasses of champagne.

''To celebrate our wedding?'' she asked, pulling up the arm rest and scooting closer to him.

He took the glasses from the attendant and handed one to Stefanie. ''No,'' he answered. ''I think this one is for your mother.''

Stefanie nodded as they clicked glasses. She and Elisabeth could never regain the years they'd lost, but just maybe they could establish something new and fine in the years they had left together.

He took her glass and put it on the lap tray in front of him, then pulled her into his arms. His kiss brushed against the side of her face and she lifted her head to meet his lips with hers.

''I love you so much it frightens me,'' Stefanie whispered. ''Without you there is no safe place on earth.''

''You'll never be without me,'' Dan promised, ''but it's because I couldn't live without you.'' The devastating force of the loneliness he'd endured these past days without her had shown him the depth of his need. He'd thought himself a solitary man, always strong, always helping others, but he knew now that it wasn't true. He needed her emotional strength, her warmth, her love, to become whole again. He needed her like he needed air and water. His feeling for her was as elemental and as all-encompassing as that.

"Settle down right here," he said, arranging the thin blanket over both of them and cradling her in his arms. "We have a long flight ahead of us and I have a lot of things I'd like to tell you."

She rested her cheek against his warm chest and settled down to learn about the man she would always love.

BARBARA BRETTON

Destiny's Child

Dakota Wylie was a typical twentieth-century woman living a typical twentieth-century life—chaotic! But it was calmer than the existence she found herself leading in eighteenth-century New Jersey with Patrick Devane. He was stubborn and cynical and thought her brazen and unladylike. But there was no denying the passion between them. Caught in a time of tumultuous change, Dakota and Patrick found their hearts on fire with hate as well as love. Now Patrick was accused of spying. And Dakota had to decide whether she had traveled two hundred years through time to lie with a man who was now branded an enemy....

Don't miss *Destiny's Child* this September, at your favorite retail outlet.

MIRA The brightest star in women's fiction   MBBDC

Take 3 of "The Best of the Best™" Novels FREE
Plus get a FREE surprise gift!

Special Limited-time Offer

Mail to The Best of the Best™

3010 Walden Avenue
P.O. Box 1867
Buffalo, N.Y. 14269-1867

YES! Please send me 3 free novels and my free surprise gift. Then send me 3 of "The Best of the Best™" novels each month. I'll receive the best books by the world's hottest romance authors. Bill me at the low price of $3.74 each plus 25¢ delivery and applicable sales tax, if any.* That's the complete price and a savings of over 10% off the cover prices—quite a bargain! I understand that accepting the books and gift places me under no obligation ever to buy any books. I can always return a shipment and cancel at any time. Even if I never buy another book from Harlequin, the 3 free books and the surprise gift are mine to keep forever.

183 BPA ANV9

Name	(PLEASE PRINT)	
Address		Apt. No.
City	State	Zip

This offer is limited to one order per household and not valid to current subscribers.
*Terms and prices are subject to change without notice. Sales tax applicable in N.Y.
All orders subject to approval.

UBOB-295

©1990 Harlequin Enterprises Limited

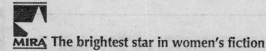

Compelling Debut Author

TAYLOR SMITH

Catapults you into a world where deception is the rule

Guilt by Silence

In the flash of an eye, Mariah Bolt's world came crashing down. Confronted by the destruction of her family and too many unanswered questions, she's determined to prove that her husband's accident was a carefully planned attempt at murder. As she probes deeper into what really happened, she realizes that she can trust no one—not the government, not her husband, not even Paul Chaney, the one person willing to help her. Because now Mariah is the target.

Available this June at your favorite retail outlet.